ALIEN STORIES

by

E.C. OSONDU

AMERICAN READER SERIES, NO. 36
BOA EDITIONS, LTD. ❖ ROCHESTER, NY ❖ 2021

First Edition
21 22 23 24 7 6 5 4 3 2 1

For information about permission to reuse any material from this book, please contact The Permissions Company at www.permissionscompany.com or e-mail permdude@gmail.com.

Publications by BOA Editions, Ltd.—a not-for-profit corporation under section 501 (c) (3) of the United States Internal Revenue Code—are made possible with funds from a variety of sources, including public funds from the Literature Program of the National Endowment for the Arts; the New York State Council on the Arts, a state agency; and the County of Monroe, NY. Private funding sources include the Max and Marian Farash Charitable Foundation; the Mary S. Mulligan Charitable Trust; the Rochester Area Community Foundation; the Ames-Amzalak Memorial Trust in memory of Henry Ames, Semon Amzalak, and Dan Amzalak; the LGBT Fund of Greater Rochester; and contributions from many individuals nationwide. See Colophon on page 176 for special individual acknowledgments.

Cover Design: Sandy Knight
Cover Art: Roslyn Rose
Interior Design and Composition: Richard Foerster
BOA Logo: Mirko

BOA Editions books are available electronically through BookShare, an online distributor offering Large-Print, Braille, Multimedia Audio Book, and Dyslexic formats, as well as through e-readers that feature text to speech capabilities.

Library of Congress Cataloging-in-Publication Data

Names: Osondu, E. C., author.
Title: Alien stories / by E. C. Osondu.
Description: First edition. | Rochester, NY : BOA Editions, Ltd., 2021. | Series: American reader series ; no. 36 | Summary: "Short Fiction Prize-winning collection of short stories that use science fiction to explore immigration, diaspora, and the concept of otherness"— Provided by publisher.
Identifiers: LCCN 2020048760 (print) | LCCN 2020048761 (ebook) | ISBN 9781950774319 (paperback) | ISBN 9781950774326 (ebook)
Subjects: LCSH: Science fiction, Nigerian (English) | LCGFT: Short stories.
Classification: LCC PR9387.9.O856 A79 2021 (print) | LCC PR9387.9.O856 (ebook) | DDC 823/.914—dc23
LC record available at https://lccn.loc.gov/2020048760
LC ebook record available at https://lccn.loc.gov/2020048761

BOA Editions, Ltd.
250 North Goodman Street, Suite 306
Rochester, NY 14607
www.boaeditions.org
A. Poulin, Jr., Founder (1938–1996)

ALIEN STORIES

Winner of the Short Fiction Prize

For my family—Evelyn, Michael, Chuchu, Cheta, CJ.

CONTENTS

9   Alien Enactors

21   Memory Store

33   How to Raise an Alien Baby

41   Visitors

51   Feast

57   Mark

65   Spaceship

76   Sacrifice

85   Light

94   Traveler

103   Debriefing

112   Focus Group

122   Child's Play

130   Who Is in the Garden?

140   On the Lost Tribes of the Black World

146   Love Affair

158   The Home Companion

163   All Our Earthly Possessions

171   *Acknowledgments*

173   *About the Author*

176   *Colophon*

Alien Enactors

The Instaratings from my previous week's enactments were stellar. At the Ranch when one received an outstanding Instarating as I just did, one figuratively walked on air. One did not need to do a Selfcrit like the others. One did not have to ask oneself seven critical questions and provide seven critical responses. Great Instaratings made one feel like a contestant in that show from long ago, *Survivor,* who did well in the team challenge and got a chance to scarf down caviar and Gruyère cheese and chilled Pinot Grigio while their opponents who lost subsisted on locust and wild honey or whatever miserable victuals losers were allowed to eat.

Not that we were allowed to gloat at the Ranch. We were one big team. We were one happy family. We were here to support each other. We would be nothing without each other. That was the whole idea: to be each other's keeper. So gloating was not allowed, but it was OK to feel good.

My duty was to enact Africa for guests, and oh boy, how they loved my act. I pulled no stops. I made each of the clients wear a colorful dashiki and I had them gather around in a circle and then encouraged them to empty their minds and get rid of their old personalities and visualize themselves sitting under an iroko tree in an African village square. I started my enactment with the obligatory proverb about how it took a village to raise a child—popularized by a female politician. Allow me to make a little confession here: in all my years growing up in Africa I had never

heard anybody use that particular proverb. Oh well . . .
different strokes and all that, but it is a cute proverb all the
same and my guests lapped it up.

I told my guests an African folktale filled with talking
animals and cruel kings and precious princesses and trem-
bling subjects. I made them sing and dance and had them
play the parts of different animals within the story. They
were all truly transported to the heart of the eternal drumbeat that was Africa.

No wonder they Instarated my enactment as outstanding.

Ling, my colleague, had received less than stellar ratings. Let us just say her ratings had been abysmal lately.
The truth hurts, right? I know. But sometimes you have to
bite the bullet, swallow the bitter pill and say the truth even
if it did not make everyone feel gruntled. Ling's fire was
dimming; at least that was what most people at the Ranch
were saying.

Ling's ratings were slipping; it was there for all to see.
In her Selfcrit, instead of asking herself the seven critical
questions and providing answers to them, she was busy
blaming the clients. She complained that her clients were
the wrong sort. She said her clients did not give her the
chance to display her creativity and expertise.

She seemed to have forgotten our Two Suggestions. As
the Suggestion Book always reminded us, these were not
rules but *suggestions* because we were free moral agents and
not mindless automatons.

Suggestion Number 1: The client is always right.

Suggestion Number 2: When in doubt, see Suggestion
Number 1 above.

I pulled up Ling on my Palm screen and typed a smi-
ley face.

Ling responded with a teary face.

I typed a sad face with a frowny mouth and sad eyes.

Ling responded with a requested that we meet in person.

I obliged.

"Chinese food, food, food, that is all they want me to talk about," she said.

She'd been crying and her heavy makeup was ruined. Her red cheongsam was all askew. She was not looking good. Still, one needs to be a good colleague and we were all one here at the Ranch and we should be our brother's or sister's keeper as the case may be.

"Ling, my Instaratings were quite low at one time, remember? They were all a little less complimentary, but I pulled myself up by the bootstraps and refused to be down at the mouth, and look at me today."

I bit back my tongue as I reminded myself not to come off as boastful or immodest. I had a responsibility to help Ling get back on her feet and be the best she could be so the Ranch would fulfill its corporate destiny and raison d'être.

"What can I do to help?" I asked.

"To be honest, I don't know. I think the problem is China. They want to talk about Chinese food. I wouldn't have a problem talking about General Tso's Chicken and Peking Duck and Sesame Chicken if that would open the door to great Instaratings, but the clients hardly give me a chance. I think some of the guests would prefer that I cook them Chinese food. The truth is, I wouldn't know how to cook the stuff if . . . You know, I don't even like Chinese food."

Ling realized she'd gone a little too far. What she'd just said verged on being too big of a *self-reveal*. This was not Selfcrit. And even in Selfcrit one was not allowed to suggest one was incompetent or less-than in any possible way. The language of Selfcrit was slanted just so, that one did not come across as a slacker.

One said stuff like: *I struggle to connect with my clients at every level sometimes.*

I am not often at my optimal cheerfulness.

I need to work really harder at being more perfect.

I need to be more fired-up.

I must become the role I play every day.

We were all colleagues at the Ranch and were all fit and competent and were the best to be found and had been found worthy in both character and learning. We were the chosen ones. It was a grievous error to admit that we were less than competent or not the best or not the peak of the pack.

I honestly wanted to help Ling.

"Look, Ling, I know how less than encouraging these less than optimal Instaratings could be, but have you considered maybe telling Chinese folktales? Chinese legends are amazing. My African folktales are usually a big hit with my clients."

"Chinese folktales? Hmm, they are not like your African stories, you know. In Chinese folktales those who do good end up being punished. No good deed ever goes unpunished."

"Ah," I said.

"Have you heard the one about the four dragons that tried to save the people of China from drought?"

"I have not, but I think dragons are cool," I said.

"Once, there was a drought, and the Chinese people were dying of starvation and thirst because there was no rain. When the four dragons heard the cries of the people, they decided to intercede on their behalf by pleading with the Jade Emperor to send down rain. The Jade Emperor said he would send down rain but promptly forgot about it. The dragons decided to get water from the sea and pour it down from the sky like rain, and when they did this, people were happy. However, when the Jade Emperor heard what the dragons had done he was furious at them for usurping his role. The Jade Emperor called down four mountains to imprison the four dragons. The four kind-hearted dragons ended up dying in their mountain prison."

"Ah," I said again, even more emphatically this time. "That one sounds a bit uncheerful."

"You see what I mean?" Ling asked.

I indeed saw what she meant, but I was not going to tell her that.

"You can always be creative with your stories, you know. I use a bit of creativity every now and again, myself," I said.

"You do?" Ling asked, sounding a little bit ominous.

I glanced awkwardly at my Palm screen.

"I see, you have to get back to work," Ling said.

I half nodded.

"I am so sorry I've been such a pest," Ling said. "I must learn to pick up after myself."

"We all have our less than optimal moments," I said.

I watched from the corner of my eyes as she schlepped away with her head bowed.

My Palm screen lit up in blue, and a message scrolled across.

You have clients. You have clients. You have clients.

I straightened up and put on my game face, or rather my Africa enactment face. I was ready to go get 'em.

I checked my Palm screen.

My heart thumped loudly. It was so hard I could hear it in my ears.

It was somewhat true what they always told us about being an enactor at the Ranch—no two clients were ever the same. This was the fun part of our calling.

"Jambo!" my client greeted me, over-cheerfully.

"Jambo!" I hailed back, slightly raising the pitch of my voice to match his high-octane enthusiasm.

He was wearing a dashiki and had a necklace made from seashells and cowrie beads around his neck. He began addressing me after shaking my hand vigorously and elaborately.

"Ah, I miss Africa. I never knew I was going to miss it until I left. I seemed to live more while I was there. Life seems to come at you in waves over there. You feel more. You know what I mean, right? More alive. More aware. More aware of the fact that every blessed moment could be your last. Boom, you are about to cross the road without looking left or right like everyone else and boom seemingly out of nowhere a *matatu* with loud music booming from its loudspeakers runs into you and boom you are on your way to meet your maker. Just like that. Boom!"

"Boom!" I said.

I sensed he was going to do all the talking, so I let him.

"That smell. You know that smell, right? There is nothing quite like that smell. The smell of Africa."

"We can make that smell happen for you right here at the Ranch," I said.

"You can?" he asked.

"Just give me one second," I said.

I gathered dry banana leaves and corn husks and built a little fire. I sprinkled a few seeds of cayenne pepper on it as soon as the leaves started burning.

He sniffed the air like a young rodent. He breathed in, then sniffed again.

"The smell, the smell. I can smell Africa again. It smells just right," he said.

"That is what the Ranch is here to do for you. We do our best to make our guests happy," I said.

"You know, unlike most people who go to Africa, I did not see myself going to Africa in the mold of some kind of *Save Africa Messiah*. I was kind of hoping to get away somewhere to save myself. I did not go with the intention of helping orphans. Don't get me wrong, helping orphans is great, and orphans, of which there are a great number in Africa, need all the help they can get. But to be honest, I could barely help me."

"There is no place like Africa," I said.

"Let me tell you this, Africa was the only place that did not judge me. I was used to being judged by family, judged in school, judged at the shitty dead-end jobs where I typically got fired after a few weeks, but Africa never judged me."

"The motherland never judges anyone," I said.

The fire was burning out. The Africa smell was fading. His time was running out. I liked guests like him. He was the one who did all the performing. Don't get me wrong, though. I did of course love to enact.

I looked at my Palm screen.

He looked at me.

"Ah, I nearly forgot myself. You don't operate on African Time here. You know, back in Africa their attitude to time was one thing that I loved about them. Their sense of time is straight out of Salvador Dali's *The Persistence of Memory*. They know something we don't know over here—time is made for man, man is not made for time."

"No truer word has ever been said."

"Speaking of which, I have to skedaddle," he said.

I thanked him as the Instarating prompt came on. I looked away like a good waiter does at tipping time.

As soon as he walked off, I checked my Instarating.

Excellent!

He'd even included an exclamation mark.

I was reluctant to admit it publicly, but there was no doubt I was on a roll. Who knows, maybe soon I would become a Leader. In the history of the Ranch none of those who enacted Africa had ever risen to become Leaders. I could be the first. Who knows? I did not dwell on these thoughts for too long. One had to watch out for shortcomings like arrogance, pride, and immodesty. It was OK to take pride in one's work but one must remember that the Ranch was all little parts working together as one. This was one of the principles that I taught my guests as being at the core of African personhood. This was what *Ubuntu* stood for. This was acknowledging that one was nothing without others. One was only a person because of other people.

It was time to clock out. I switched off my Palm screen. Of course, everyone knew the Palm screen never really went off and never stops watching you.

At the dining hall that night, I was the object of all manners of accolades. Other performers slapped my back. From every corner of the hall my fellow enactors called out to me.

"Africa rising," some said.

"Black power," some called out.

"Africa on top," another said.

"Africa on the move," yet another called out in greeting.

There were questions from all sides.

"Can you tell us how you do it?"

"What is the secret of your success?"

"What can I do to improve?"

I smiled and remembered that one needed to be modest especially with fellow enactors because everyone at the Ranch was a person because of everyone else. I reined in the surge of pride growing in my chest and put on my modest face.

"I could not have done it without you, my fellow enactors. If I am standing tall today, you all know what they say, right? It is because I'm standing on the shoulders of my fellow enactors. We are all enacting great continents. We just need to make our clients connect with our beloved continents and watch those ratings go stratospheric."

"Great speech," they said.

"Morale-boosting speech," they said.

"Hear, hear," they said.

I scanned the length and breadth of the dining hall for Ling. She was sitting by herself in a corner. She was like the unpopular kid in high school who sat alone during lunch and had serial killing in their future.

I could see her dinner on her Styrofoam plate. It was a single baby carrot. She was having a single baby carrot for lunch. She needed her morale boosted. She needed a pep talk. She needed a puff of air beneath her wings. Who better to give it than the man who'd just made a great morale-boosting speech? However, as I walked towards her lonely table, she stood up and walked away, her eyes on the grotty floor.

I asked myself a bunch of questions.

Had I somehow hurt her by being immodest?

Had I been less than supportive to my fellow enactor?

Had I done anything to make her feel a little less about her personhood?

No, No, and No.

Since the answers to all three questions were negative, I proceeded to enjoy my dinner heartily.

❖

My Palm screen told me I had clients. They were a mixed group so I decided to give them my *Tell me something I don't know about Africa* routine.

"Do you know that in some parts of Africa people are buried in coffins made in the shape of their professions?" I asked them.

I then answered my own question.

"A doctor's coffin would be shaped like a stethoscope and a lawyer's like a wig and gown and a mechanic's would be shaped like a spanner and a musician's is shaped like a guitar."

Their responses ranged from *wow* to *cool,* etc., etc.

One of the clients, a college kid, raised his hand to ask a question. For some reason, questions made me somewhat apprehensive. Had I not been thorough enough in my presentation?

"What about the coffin-maker?"

"Yes, the coffin-maker," I said.

"When the coffin-maker dies, is he buried in a coffin-shaped coffin because his profession is coffin-making?"

A few people laughed. Not good laughter. More like gotcha laughter.

"Well, technically, a coffin-maker is a carpenter so he gets buried in either a hand-plane or a saw-shaped coffin," I said.

My answer sounded satisfactory to my clients.

The Instarating prompt came on and they all set about rating me.

When they left, I checked. They'd all awarded me Excellent.

Later that evening all of the enactors gathered for a Groupcrit. Our Leader gave his usual speech telling us to have the right attitude to Groupcrits. We should embrace the opportunity that Groupcrits offered us to become better enactors. There was no doubt that those who performed best were those who saw Groupcrits as a way to improve their performance. He looked pointedly at me, nodded, and cracked a tiny, little smile.

I smiled back broadly.

He nodded at Ling. He did not smile.

Ling stood up.

From every corner of the hall voices rose at Ling. She looked thinner and frailer than she used to. Her eyes were red from crying.

"I know I have not been pulling my own weight these past few weeks but I promise to do my best to improve," she mumbled.

"Promises are not good enough. Promises are nothing without practical applications," our Leader said.

"Am I right, enactors?"

"Promises are nothing," we echoed.

One by one, individual voices rose from different corners of the hall.

"By not pulling your own weight you are pulling the Ranch down."

"You are dead weight."

"The Ranch is as strong as its weakest link."

The Leader nodded and smiled, and this no doubt increased the tempo and furiousness of the enactors as their criticisms came on fast and furious.

"You are bringing us down."

"You are not working as part of a team."

"You are lowering team morale."

"You are not doing enough for China."

"You are doing China a disservice."

The Leader, meanwhile, paced. He was pacing through the four corners of the hall as the criticisms rained down. His head was up, but his eyes looked at no one, they looked straight ahead.

"I can see that we all agree promises are not enough. The Ranch is standing today because we all pull together. We cannot allow any lone individual to pull us down. I need time to think."

He walked out of the hall with his hands behind his back.

The rest of us began to troop out. I did not look at Ling. I had to be careful not to be seen as joining myself with an enactor who was pulling the Ranch down.

The next morning I did a welfare check on Ling but her face didn't come up on my Palm screen. Where her face should have been, there was a black spot. This could only mean one thing—her fire had gone out.

I shook my head, but only for a brief moment. I remembered a common saying at the Ranch—*enactors come, enactors go, but the Ranch remains.*

As I looked at Ling's black spot, I resolved to work even harder to maintain my excellent Instaratings.

Memory Store

One of the things he found most fascinating about America were the Memory Stores that could be found on almost every street corner. A person could simply walk into any of the stores and sell their memories for money. It was that straightforward. He had come to the realization that certain things were undoubtedly straightforward in America. Take American beers with their twist-off caps. Twist-off caps may not seem like a big deal to most American beer drinkers but he remembered buying a cold bottle of beer when he was back home and bringing it to his room and ransacking the entire room in search of his bottle opener. He eventually found the opener lying underneath a pile of old newspapers. By then, the beer was already lukewarm and tasted flat on the tongue.

Even in matters that did not appear so straightforward, he still admired America. He loved the fact that in America there were a dozen different kinds of doughnuts. There were even doughnuts without holes. Back home, he had grown up knowing only one kind of doughnut: light brown with a hole in the center. He recalled his first time in an American doughnut shop.

"I want a doughnut," he said to the sales clerk.

"Which one of them do you want?" she asked.

He had pointed vaguely in the direction of the glass display case. The sales clerk looked at him and began pointing out and reeling off the names of the different kinds of doughnuts that they had.

"Glazed, Chocolate, Vanilla Frosted, Powdered Sugar, Old Fashioned . . ."

Looking at her, he had pointed at the light brown doughnut with a hole in the middle.

"Honey, you mean *Old Fashioned*? Why didn't you say so instead of messing with me?"

She sounded relieved and laughed.

The coffee-laden atmosphere had lightened. He too had laughed. He had repeated the words "Old Fashioned" and had vowed to commit it to memory.

A Memory Store, ah, only in America. He planned to visit one and find out how it worked. He had no immediate plans to sell his memories but there was no harm in knowing about their operations. He was sure the operators of the Memory Stores would be as polite and pleasant as he had found most American storekeepers to be. Here in America even when a storekeeper did not have an item that you wished to buy he would direct you to another store where they had the item, sometimes at an even cheaper rate. That would never happen back home. The best a shopkeeper would do for you would be to tell you to wait while he dashed to a neighboring store to get the same item and sell it to you with a markup.

The first time he went into a Memory Store he walked in furtively like a Catechist walking into a brothel. First he looked right, then left and then right again and then he ducked in.

As soon as he entered the shop, all his apprehensions disappeared.

"Hi, buddy, I am R," the guy who manned the shop said.

He in turn introduced himself by his first initial.

Everyone went by their initials these days. It was one

of the laws introduced to unite the country after what had happened during the previous regime.

He could tell that the man was Hispanic. He could tell from the man's accent. You could not get rid of accents by a simple legislation. Did the R. stand for Ramos, Ramirez, Rodriguez? It was inappropriate to ask. Such things did not matter anymore. Everyone was American and that was all that was important.

"It is very easy, my friend," the guy said

He had looked around the store. He had expected to see lots of gadgets but there were actually just a few.

"First, I will need to wipe down your hands with rubbing alcohol and then you'll place the five fingers of both hands on this glass panel in front of me and then you'll focus your mind and recall the memory you want to sell to us. Your memory will appear on the screen right here and I will tell you how much we are able to pay for it. If we agree on the price then I will give you a card loaded with the amount for which we bought your memory. You can use the card to make purchases anywhere. There are stores down the road from here, they sell good stuff. The process is painless," R. explained.

He told R. that he had only come to look around and find out how the thing worked.

"Look around, my friend. Take your time and feel free to ask me if you have any questions," R. said.

He looked around but there really wasn't much more to see than what R. had showed him. It looked like a pretty basic operation. Just then the bell rang announcing the arrival of a customer. R. showed him out through another door.

He looked forward to his job. He worked with Work Ready. They provided workers for the car auction. They provided both drivers and cleaners. He was one of the cleaners.

His job was to wash the cars and wipe them down and make them look good on the auction block. The thought that a car that he had tidied would be driven by a man who lived in a far-off place such as one of the Gulf States thrilled him and made him shine the cars with gusto.

His boss had stood watching him one day while he used a clean, dry piece of cloth to shine a car he had just washed. He had looked up and seen his boss watching him.

"I have never seen anyone wipe down a car with so much joy," his boss said.

"I always do a good job because you never know where the cars might end up," he said to his boss.

"You never know, huh? Good job, keep it up," his boss had said.

He had thanked his boss.

His boss had made to walk away and then had come back and said to him, "You know there can only be one supervisor here, right? I've been the supervisor for three years and the company has no plans to fire me or promote any person to my position. Still, I like your hustle, man."

The short speech had left him confused but he had only smiled and continued with his cleaning.

Later that winter he had reported at Work Ready one morning and was met by the long faces of his colleagues. Work Ready was letting the cleaners go. They were *consolidating*—that was the language they used. The drivers would be the ones to clean the cars from now onwards. It was a way to save money.

His supervisor had pulled him aside to the hallway near the bathroom and had asked him if he could drive. He had said he couldn't. The supervisor had told him to go to a driving school and to come back when he got his driver's license.

He sat before the Memory Machine and began to dredge

his mind. He realized how true something he had heard years ago was: everything in life becomes difficult when you try to force it. He thought that since his mind often wandered into the past recalling stuff would be easy. His mind was going blank at the moment.

"Some people find that when they close their eyes, it helps," R. said to him.

He closed his eyes and hoped he would not nod off and start snoring loudly. Why was he worrying about everything all of a sudden?

His mind became clear. The fog lifted. He was a little boy of seven running home from school. He could still smell the aroma of jollof rice and fried goat meat. At the completion of the academic year, they were served jollof rice and fried goat meat by the school. He didn't wait for the jollof rice or the fried goat meat. He snatched his report card as soon as they announced that he was the first in his class and began to run home to his grandmother.

She was outside bathing in the sun. She was wearing her green sweater, the one with the Christmas decorations. His grandmother didn't know that the design on her sweater was Christmas decorations. He wouldn't know either until he came to America. He would also learn in America that they were called "ugly sweaters." He never did understand why. They were beautifully colorful to him.

He handed the report card to his grandmother.

"Tell me what it says, my son."

"Open it, grandma. Look at it yourself," he said to her.

"You open it and read it to me, that is why I sent you to school," she said.

He opened the report card and told her that he came first in his class and that he had scored one hundred percent in all his subjects and that he had not stayed back to eat the jollof rice and goat meat that was cooked for all the students for the end of the academic year.

"Will their jollof rice taste as good as the one I am going to make for you?" his grandmother asked.

"Never," he said.

R. was tapping him on the shoulder. He was almost too far gone. So carried away by the memory that he had forgotten where he was and had been transported entirely into that world of his childhood with his grandmother.

"That is all we'll need for today's session. You did really great. These types are quite rare. They've got everything we are looking for in a memory. Genuine, not artificial, and filled with joy. Now follow me and I'll give you your payment. It is a card. It is loaded and you can use it at designated stores to buy really good stuff," R. said.

He was still feeling a little unfocused from the experience. For some reason he was also feeling lighter, but not in a heavy-load-taken-away kind of way; it was like he had misplaced something—perhaps an object he had in his pocket had been lost.

He collected the payment card. He was surprised at the amount they were paying him.

"Thank you," he said to R.

"No, thank *you*," R. said.

He hesitated to leave. Something was still bothering him. It had all seemed too easy.

"So what is going to happen to the one I just gave you?" he asked R.

"We are going to put it to good use. Like I told you, it is a great one. Very much in high demand. Authentic and genuine. They are gonna love it."

"Ah," he said.

"You know some people come here and try to sell us

fake memories or pass off other people's memories as their own, but the machine has a system for detecting those kinds real quick," R. said.

"The one I just gave you, what about it?" he asked.

"Oh, I see what you mean. It is gone. You will never recall that particular memory again. It is like it never existed. Wiped out. Gone. It no longer belongs to you. But don't worry about it. I am sure there are lots where that came from, buddy," R. said. R. sounded jokey but a little furtive in his manner. He could tell that R. wanted him to leave.

He took his card and walked to the store that sold household goods. He had always wanted a huge television. He wanted a giant one that would dominate the environment of his sitting room. The lives of American families did not revolve around the television the way lives did back home. Back home the television had come to replace the grandmother around whom everybody sat after the evening meal listening as she told her folktales. Over here the television was overlooked just like American grandmothers who talked to themselves for the most part and who went largely ignored when they spoke to other occupants of the house. Life here rather revolved around the fridge. The opening of the fridge and the slamming of the fridge door and the perpetual complaint of "there is nothing to eat; there is never anything to eat here" though the fridge would usually be bursting from the seams with all kinds of food and drink.

He bought the giant television. It was sixty-four inches. They took it home for him. He rode with the delivery guys and watched them install it. He sat in front of the television and began flipping channels. He flipped and flipped again, his right hand and thumb feeling heavy, yet there still remained channels to flip.

He recalled that back home the television came on at 4 p.m. That was when the station opened. The station closed at 11 p.m. There was hardly more than an hour of movies and drama—the rest of the time was devoted to men and women in elaborate costume-like clothes using big words to argue between themselves about how to move the country forward.

He stumbled on a soccer game and stopped.

There was no commentary.

It must have been originally in Spanish but had been edited to remove the Spanish commentary. They had not bothered to do the work of substituting an English language commentary.

He began to watch the game without commentary by following the colors of the jerseys of the players. His eyes soon grew weary and he fell asleep and began to snore. The television was still on and soon was watching him sleep. It was one of the modern types of TV and when it sensed no movement in the sitting room it shut itself down. When he woke up he was sitting in the dark, alone without the television glow, but he was not afraid of the darkness here in America. He found American darkness to be somewhat more gray than dark. Back home he would stretch out his hands while walking in the dark and even his hand disappeared and became one with the inky darkness.

He went to Work Ready to ask if there were job openings. The lady there told him that they were giving priority to people who were mandated to work by a judge so that they could pay their child support.

"We are focused on placing those who have to pay their child support, right now. Others will just have to wait," she said.

He had asked after the supervisor who had asked that

he get in touch as soon as he could drive and was told that the supervisor had resigned. So if he had paid money to go to a driving school as the guy had suggested, it would have been for nothing?

He told the lady he would look in some other time. She said sure thing, that he should keep checking in with them from time to time.

He decided to head to the Memory Store.

He went through the routine. Wiped his hands down. He worked on coming up with a memory. It was easier this time around. He had gone to play soccer with the brand new Wembley soccer ball that his grandmother had bought for him. He had enjoyed the pleasure of picking those who were going to play on his side as the owner of the soccer ball. The game had been fun all the way with both sides scoring two goals each. Then when they were taking a break prepara- tory to changing sides one of the big boys who had been watching the game from the sides, his name was Monday, asked to join the game. He had said No. Monday seized the soccer ball saying that if they would not let him play then they could not play either and that the ball would not be given back. He had tried to get his ball back but had re- ceived a swift kick on the shin from Monday. He had run home crying to his grandma. His grandma had sent him back to get his ball telling him not to come home without it.

R. was tapping him on the shoulder.

"This one is not good. We cannot pay for this one," R. said.

"Why, what is wrong with it?" he asked.

"Nothing is wrong with it. It is just that we don't find this type useful. People are not interested in this. It is some- what generic, if you know what I mean. Someone gets his ball stolen by a bully and he fights to get it back. Think of something else. Go to that room over there, get a cup of coffee or a ginger ale. Try and relax for a few minutes and I am sure something useful will come to you, OK," he said.

He went into the room and poured himself some ginger ale and added ice. He felt like someone who had failed his exams. What could be so hard about coming up with some good memories? But why did the store not have a list of memory items that they accepted and those that they didn't?

He sipped the ginger ale and told himself to calm down. He had not liked ginger ale as a kid. He thought it tasted too much like an adult drink. It was not sugary enough, not like the other kinds of soft drinks. As an adult in America it had become his favorite drink. He liked the austere taste.

His mind became clear and he remembered the day before he left for America. Yes, that should be a good memory. He left his half-drunk cup of ginger ale on the table and went to meet R.

"I see you are ready to try again, my friend. Let's do it," R. said.

He remembered his last day before he traveled to America. The house was filled with more people than it was accustomed. There was food and lots of it. People were eating and drinking and talking. In the background there was music playing aloud. He was not quite sure who the musician was. For some reason he remembered the title of the song. It was called "Ace."

His grandmother had refused to eat and was crying. He had told her to stop crying, that today was a happy day. She held on to his hand and repeated the words he had just said to her. She had paused and then resumed with the crying.

"I am not leaving forever. I am going to come back soon and when I come back I will build you a bigger house," he said to his grandmother.

She had stopped crying to listen to him.

"Not even your grandmother knows the secret of living forever," she said and continued to cry.

He decided to change tack since this approach was not working.

"I don't want to remember you like this. I don't want my last memory of you to be your weeping face," he said.

This seemed to have touched her and she had wiped her face with her headscarf and asked for some food and drink.

"Perfect, see I told you to take a break that you'd come up with something that we can use. It worked. This is a good one. Here, take your card. You did a good job," R. said to him.

He bought a fridge with the card. It was a gray fridge with double doors. It had a different compartment for every item. He had always thought that every fridge must come in a white color, but had been thrilled by the fact that they came in all kinds of colors these days. He had told the guys who delivered the new fridge to take away the old one but they refused. They said it was against company regulations. He had told them that it was free and that they could sell it for money since it was still working and in good condition, but they had said no. So the old fridge sat mutely beside the new one like an unwanted guest.

It was the 26th of December. It was the anniversary of the passing of his grandmother. He thought that even in her choice of the day of her death, his grandmother had been her good old considerate self—the day after Christmas was hard to forget.

He sat before his television. He had turned it off. The fridge was humming distinctly but unobtrusively.

He wanted to spend some time thinking of his grandmother and honoring her memory. He sat still and tried to picture her gentle, smiling face.

He drew a blank.

He could not remember his grandmother's face. Nothing was coming to mind.

He panicked a little. But he recalled what had happened at the Memory Store. He opened the fridge and poured himself some ginger ale into a cup and added ice. He sat down and took a sip.

He thought hard.

His grandmother's face did not come up.

There was nothing.

How to Raise an Alien Baby

Rules are rules. They exist for a reason. They are meant to be obeyed.

If, for instance, you are going to adopt or foster an earthling child you have to obey certain rules. Yes, certain requirements must be met. Your home must be clean, at least on the day of the inspection. You must be at least 21 years old, because babies can't look after babies. You must have some source of gainful employment. Why would you think fostering an alien baby is any different? The rules ought to be even more stringent, really. It is good manners to host visitors as you would family, or perhaps even better.

The first thing to know about taking care of alien babies is that you must have a large, well-manicured lawn. What for, you ask? Well, sooner or later an alien baby must return to its mother planet and the mode of transportation to that planet is the mother ship. It is expected of you to know that and keep it in mind. You are the alien baby's earth mom, it has many other mothers elsewhere. So yes, on the subject of lawns: keep it freshly mown with well-trimmed edges so that when that mother ship arrives—silently in the night, with its deep unearthly glow—you will not be ashamed when your neighbors come out of their houses, wearing robes and shoddy slippers. Even drowsy eyes can pick up a mess. You will not be ashamed by the photographs in the newspapers. Your lawn should be photogenic, prepared for media coverage.

Another rule: your house must not have any satellite dishes. You know those things that look like turned out giant's ears, eavesdropping into every terrestrial and non-terrestrial conversation? Those are a no-no. Studies have shown that even unused and abandoned dishes retain their pings. This is a well-known phenomenon in Rocket Science: even when satellites die their pings do not. You don't want your alien baby using your house as a transmission center for sending messages back to his mother planet. Though we welcome the alien baby we would prefer to keep communication to a minimum. Always remember: country first, our planet first.

And remember this too: no television antennas either. Perhaps a close friend or family member installed those for you? Perhaps they fell to their death in the act. Now is not the time for a moment of silence. If you would like to commemorate the many who have fallen while installing those spiky, dozen-fingered blighters, please take that moment at a later time. Those antennas are useful for sending back information to mother planets. Our alien guests will grab and twist every antenna-finger to tell their people sensitive things about us, if we let them. If they are living with you they will certainly know all sorts of things about you. They will know your favorite cereal—whether you are a sweet cereal type or a cheerless, unsweetened, heart-healthy kind of person. They will know about your bowel movements too, how regular you are and if you tend to get discombobulated when you feel backed up. Yes, of course they'll know all that stuff, you probably don't want an entire planet knowing these things.

But that is not what we are talking about here; we are talking serious business. Let's say we plan to attack their planet tomorrow, to seize it and make it our own, to force them to come harvest our potatoes, our almonds and tomatoes, our oranges and grapes, and so on and so forth. As you well know, in warfare, surprise attack is the mother of victory. So here we are, planning to strike with the utmost surprise, and your house guest—your innocent alien baby gets a hold of this information and decides to give his people a heads up. What do you think they'd do if they get this actionable piece of information? Of course they would strike our planet. And you bet they wouldn't show mercy. Before you know it, they've annexed our home—our dear mother Earth—and taken us to their red, dusty planet and forced us to break rocks all day while we sing "By the Rivers of Babylon." Please, no antennas on your roof.

You must also be sensitive in your choice of entertainment. You don't want to go about hurting the feelings of our little alien baby. No Syfy channel on your TV please. And none of your old DVDs and space-themed movies from yesteryear. You know the ones I'm talking about. Those boxed-up video cassettes in the basement: *Star Trek, Star Wars, Space 1999, Planet of the Apes, Logan's Run.* Get rid of them, every single one. It would be regrettable, if peradventure they stumble upon them. You don't want your guest seeing itself through your eyes. Think about their feelings. Do you realize that most of these movies—yes, most—never portray aliens as kind and generous and loving? Well, some do, but they are mostly portrayed as humorless savages, creepy and wide-eyed, just braying, "Take me to your leader."

You should know that your baby will experience . . . perhaps we don't have the word for it. Surely, the Germans do—they have a word for everything. I am talking about nostalgia for the mother planet, otherworldly homesickness.

Your alien baby will definitely get this feeling sometimes, no matter how much of a good earth parent you try to be. Don't worry too much about it. It is in no way a commentary on your parenting skills. What your alien baby needs is simply for you to sit them down and gently sing this folk song:

> *Papa went to the market eeya*
> *Mama went to the market eeya*
> *Papa will buy some savory moin-moin*
> *Mama will buy some savory akara*
> *On their return I will say Papa welcome*
> *On their return I will say Mama welcome*
> *And we shall feast igomiligo*
> *And we shall feast igomiligo*

By the time you are done your alien baby will be fast asleep, snoring slightly, an odd, peaceful smile on his face.

What kind of atmosphere do you need for your alien ward to thrive? Think of your alien baby as a fruit. Grapes need a certain type of weather and soil to do well. Alien babies, contrary to what you might think, do not require any kind of special climate, so please, do not interfere with the room temperature. No air conditioning, no fan. The occasional mild breeze should do the trick. Just keep your home free of dust mites and dander, and any furry dust balls that might trigger a sneezing fit. You probably don't know this, but here is a useful fact: when alien babies start sneezing, nothing can stop them except the finely ground feathers of the alien bird *Okanukapi*. When you touch the feather dust ever so lightly, patting their nose three times, the sneezing will stop. But how many people have *Okanukapi* feathers in their medicine cabinet? If you keep your house free of dust, you'll both breathe easier.

What kind of games should you play with your alien baby, you ask? Definitely not hide-and-seek. They can hide, but when you seek them you can never find them. When you get tired of seeking and plead for them to come out, they won't come. Soon it will no longer be a game and you may need to go to the authorities. Follow-the-leader is also out because they will always follow the leader. They don't know how not to follow the leader. You will never stop playing, you will be old and gray and still in the same game of follow-the-leader. More on this later, but just let's avoid it for now. Tag is not such a good idea either because being called "It" is not good for an alien's self-esteem.

Another question you may have: what to feed an alien baby? Mars Bars, of course! But corny jokes aside, what on Earth do alien babies eat? You can feed alien babies practically anything. They have the constitution of an ox.

While we're on the subject, you'll be relieved to know that an alien baby is very much like a self-cleaning oven. They do not need a daily bath. You need not towel them dry, nor powder their necks. They are low maintenance babies. The dreaded stinky diaper is not something you need to worry about. Alien babies are pretty much self-contained. They have an industrial blender where their alimentary canal should be.

Here's what you need to worry about, though: play dates. Unfortunately, alien babies don't play well with others. There is something about them that unnerves our Earth babies. It is something the Earth babies sense instinctively. They immediately begin to point and yell. It's like they're looking at something crazy! Like a dog with two heads. They usually don't stop yelling until their moms remove them from the scene. This is strange since Earth babies are not ordinarily a discriminating group, but there we have it. A quiet neighborhood without Earth babies would be an ideal location to raise your alien baby.

In what faith should you raise your alien baby? This is a really complicated question. The truth is that no one knows whether aliens have souls. Many theologians have spent years examining this question from different angles. Many have asked, *If aliens do not have souls, does that mean they do not sin? If they do not sin, does that mean there are no heavenly consequences for their actions? If there are no heavenly consequences, then should we take it upon ourselves, sinners that we are, to hold them accountable for any violent acts they may commit?* This is like asking whether there is more sand under the sea than in the desert. Of what use are such questions? Have you exhausted the sand in the desert? Teach them to help an old lady cross the road, to raise their hat when a lady passes by, to never spit on the street, to pause when a funeral procession goes past, to say "Yes, sir" and "Yes, ma'am." Teach them to never look down at any individual with disdain or look up to any fellow in fear. The alien will never be human. You are bound to fail but here's the good thing—an alien child never forgets what he's been taught.

While our emphasis here is more practical, we will grant that you do have a certain responsibility in this direction. You shouldn't just abandon the baby and run off to church, or the mosque, temple, ashram, or meditation center. Just teach them to worship in the way you worship. Look at the world we live in today. Very few follow the religion in which they were raised. Don't worry that your ward may proselytize, return to their little planet up there and try to convert their kin to their new faith. All the things of Earth belong to Earth and the things of space belong in space. What do they bow down to? How many times a day do they pray?

And if they do not pray at all, has it made them any worse or better than humankind?

It is impossible to raise a child without having to discipline them. As we all know, discipline comes in different forms: the raised voice, the reprimand, the ruler on the knuckle, the time-out, the confiscation of electronics, the demand for an apology. These are the most dreaded aspects of parenting that neither parent nor child look forward to. But you do not have to worry about this because your alien child does not need you to discipline them. They will never break the rules. Yes, that is a fact and you can take it to the bank. You are never going to catch your alien ward with his hand in the cookie jar, literally or metaphorically. They will not sass you back or slam the door.

This might surprise you. Some parents have even found this fact to be frustrating, and have actually started to wish that their ward *would* break the rules. Some even look for ways to make them break the rules so they can feel they are actually fulfilling their parental duty. Indeed, many have concluded that their only real function as parents is to correct their children when they stray from the straight and narrow path. It comes as a surprise to them when they discover that alien children don't need to be disciplined. Their society follows a strict command and obedience structure, you see.

Sit, you tell them, and they sit.

Do not ever open that door, you say, and they'll never touch it.

Always tuck in your shirt, you say, and they always will.

Always say please and thank you, and they'll say it without fail.

Always tidy your bed when you wake up in the morning. They will tidy their bed without fail.

Don't forget to always keep that door closed, and they never forget.

Alien babies know how to obey rules. They thrive on rules. The worst thing that you can tell an alien baby is that they are free to do as they like. Do not be surprised if they beg you to tell them what to do. Free will makes us human and it is the absence of free will that makes an alien an alien. For them, the chain of command is important. An alien child is never going to test boundaries or try to see how far they can push you. You set the rules. Tell them what to do, and how to do it.

Finally the day comes. You always knew it would, though you didn't realize that it would come so soon. Your alien ward must return to their mother planet. The ship lands on your well-manicured lawn. Your eyes grow misty, but perhaps it's just your seasonal allergies, triggered by the freshly cut grass. Your alien baby runs to the spacecraft. You linger at your front door. You wave, and they wave back. You watch the door close. The spacecraft takes off. You wave again, and keep waving at your alien baby until the spacecraft has completely disappeared. Your hands do not feel tired. You feel no ache and so you close your eyes and continue to wave.

Visitors

So my wife in her typical do-gooder fashion has volunteered to host this new alien family that moved to my little village. People have been talking about them ever since they moved into our village. Almost every person who lives here was born here and we never leave. There is nothing special about our village though we love it. We still wonder why anyone would move here. Like I said, people asked questions about them:

"Why did they decide to move here? Not that there is anything wrong with our village, but if I were an alien looking for a place to move to, this wouldn't be my first choice. Don't get me wrong, there is nothing the matter with our village in my humble opinion."

"They should have moved to a big city. It is quite easy to hide in a big city. Not that I think they have any reason to hide, but you never know. There are not many of us here and it is quite easy to stick out."

"We're all like family here. We all know each other, both the good and the bad. We know those who steal and the drunkards and those who have a family history of deafness in the left ear. But this new family? We know absolutely nothing about them."

As for me I think I know more about zombies than I know about these new guys and where they are from. I can tell you five things about zombies without even pausing: zombies have no minds of their own, they move in groups, they all look shabby, they are ugly, and there is a zombie apocalypse in mankind's future somewhere.

Now ask me to tell you a single thing about these new guys and where they come from. Go ahead ask me. See, I have no answer. I know nothing about them. *Nada*. Zilch.

So, back to my wife. She is a good woman but the problem is that she is too good for her own good, sometimes. She does not think that there is any person's problem that should be left to that person to resolve on their own. No, my wife must take on the problem herself and would not rest until the problem is gone. She sees nothing wrong in adding all these problems to our own heavy load.

Is someone sick, in hospital, feeling unwell in any way?

Trust my wife to rush down to the person with different pills in different plastic containers offering them medications. In addition she would go with a flask of hot water and sachets of Milo and milk and sugar asking them to drink and feel warm.

Is there a family that is bereaved? She would be the first to be there and she will have some beautiful thing to say about the departed person:

"Oh, no, never again shall we see someone who smiled as warmly as he did."

"Each time I met her she always said something that made me smile."

"She loved to share and would give you the very dress on her back not minding if she walked home naked."

"He treated everyone like they were his blood relations."

"He looked so strong the last time I saw him. Ah, death is indeed evil."

And so forth and so on.

My wife once took in a stray cat, too. Now, this ugly old gray cat had everything wrong with it. It was going blind in one eye. It had a limp. It was mean-spirited and never purred, but sat there with one half-shut eye looking moody and offended. Now this cat, no matter how many times my wife tried to make it stay, would run back into the woods behind our house. My wife would feed it condensed milk and the cat would lap it up, but once my wife turned her face the cat would run back into the woods and only come back during lunch time for free food and condensed milk. I nicknamed the vile rogue Old Moocher.

"Can't you see that the cat does not wish to stay? Can't you see that the cat is just using you? It likes the free food but also wants to do what it likes with itself," I said.

"The cat needs to get used to human love once again," my wife said.

Whenever it got cold or was drizzling or threatening to rain, Old Moocher would saunter in as if it owned the house. As soon as the weather warmed up, there was nothing you could do to entice it to come into the house.

"This blighter of a cat is using you. Can't you see that?" I asked my wife.

"We just need to be a little patient with him. You'll see. We need to feed him with love."

"Some love indeed. Even your condensed milk is wasted on him," I said.

Old Moocher and I avoided each other. He was wary around me and flinched whenever I came close to him. For some reason he never wandered in when I was the only one in the house. I wondered what he was running away from. I thought they were reputed to have nine lives.

Anyway, one fine day, my wife waited for Old Moocher to show up but he didn't turn up that day or the day after. That was the last we saw of him. I wish I could say that there wasn't a dry eye in the house.

My wife was heartbroken, though. She kept saying that we had failed him. We failed him, indeed, I thought. Most likely he had found better tasting condensed milk elsewhere.

Yes, back to the new family. People continued to ask questions of them:

"How did you hear about our little village that made you move here?"

"Has our reputation grown so wide that people outside have heard of us?"

"How long do you plan to stay here?"

The questions wouldn't stop. But they meant no mischief. It was the same way an old maid who suddenly finds herself deluged with marriage proposals from good-looking suitors would feel and respond.

It came as no surprise to me when I heard that my wife had invited them to our house. She would host Lucifer himself if she got a chance. I am not in any way suggesting that the aliens were like good old Lucifer. Just saying.

"You should have told me that you were going to invite them to the house. Not for nothing, but we both live in this house and if you are going to host some aliens you should at least give me a heads up," I said to her.

"Of what use were you in the past when I hosted other people?" she asked.

"Are you saying I should go hide in the closet while they are here?" I asked.

"You will do no such thing. You will be polite and pleasant to them while they are here. You'll do everything to make their visit a good one," she said.

I could tell that she meant it. One thing about my wife, she may be soft when it came to cats and aliens but when it came to dealing with me she sure knew how to crack that whip.

I decided to change my approach when I realized my first tack was not working.

"Remember your African friends and how nice I was to them?"

Now, she was smiling. Was it my question that was making her smile, or the memory of her African friends? I could never be sure with her. This was what bothered me about our relationship—this quality she had of making me feel like a second-grader squirming in front of the teacher's desk and raising his finger to indicate number one or number two.

"You were not nice to them initially, if I recall correctly," she said.

How on earth could I have been nice to them? What did I know of Africa and Africans? When she had mentioned that we were going to have visitors from Africa, the first thing that had occurred to me was the movie I had seen about Africa years ago. In the movie there was this wizened guy who was very meagerly clothed following a Coca Cola bottle to the ends of the earth. The Coke bottle was carelessly thrown out of a chopper and had unsettled the hitherto tranquil life of this man and his family and the rugged fellow had decided that he would return it to whoever had thrown this bottle of discord into his family.

I had watched the movie so many times, and each time I watched it I would scream at the man to chill and go back home, that it was only a fucking soda bottle.

What else did I know about Africa?

I knew that it was the birth place of Freddie Mercury. I loved Queen. I loved their song "The Great Pretender." I loved "Bohemian Rhapsody."

But guess what: these aliens from the African continent had turned out to be not too bad, actually. The African wife immediately followed my wife to the kitchen and began to cut, dice, cook, fry, and soon enough a beautiful aroma that I didn't know my kitchen was capable of producing began to emerge from there.

The husband sat with their young alien son in the sitting room with me and we began to watch football. I assumed he didn't know anything about the game, but he told me that he understood the game and that he had actually signed his son up for Pop Warner though the boy had not played flag. He said his son loved the game, but was not a good player, but wanted to impress his dad like a good boy. He said on this cold day they had gone to play a game in another town. Something he said about the coach: he said the coach was very strict and had warned the parents that on no account were they ever to run into the field of play during games.

On this day his son had jumped up to catch the ball, no doubt playing to impress his father, but he missed and fell, hitting his head on the ground. Another player picked up the ball and then they noticed the boy was down. The father could not run into the field to find out what was wrong with his son. He watched as the unconscious boy was stretchered out of the field. He had run to where his son was lying on the stretcher and had touched the boy's face. The son had opened his eyes that minute and had asked the father if the game was over.

I enjoyed his story. The father's anguish, clearly evident as he told the story, made me realize that Africans were people like me, too. We had all enjoyed the wife's cooking and I had told them to come back and visit whenever they felt like it.

Eventually our alien visitors arrived. They had a little son who looked barely a year old. I was beginning to notice the fact that aliens always had children. I welcomed

them and smiled even wider than I was used to smiling—
so much so my cheeks began to feel strained.

I had to ask them what everyone in our little village had
always wanted to ask.

"So why did you guys choose to settle here of all places?"

"You don't have to answer any of his questions if you
don't feel like it," my wife interjected.

"Oh, no, not a problem at all," the alien man said.

My wife smiled and went to the kitchen and came back
with cupcakes and orange juice for their little son. She explained that she was cooking up something for the adults.

"Actually he cannot have any of the cake. He was just
discharged from the hospital recently. If you have some
white grape juice or apple juice, that'd be fine," the wife
said apologetically.

The alien guy had not answered my question, so I repeated it. He seemed like a nice guy after all.

"Yes, sorry—I wasn't ignoring you," he said. "I was just
trying to remember how we arrived at our choice of this
place. Yes, so we had this map of the United States and we
placed a coin in the middle and rolled it, and when the coin
came to a stop, it rested on your village. So we knew that
this was going to be our destination."

I examined his face to see if he was joking, but he looked
serious though there was a hint of a smile on his face.

"Met your match," my wife said to me with glee.

His wife handed their little son to the man and went to
the basement with my wife to look at the clothes and toys
she had packed for them.

I looked at the little boy: he was calm but seemed tired.
I knew kids his age loved to crawl around and pull things
down and stick their little chubby fingers into stuff. This
kid looked quiet.

"Your son is so quiet," I said.

"He's been very sick. He just got discharged from the hospital not long ago," the father said.

To be honest it came as some kind of shock to me that this alien kid had fallen sick. I thought they were immune to such things. Thankfully, I had the self-control not to utter all my thoughts; it was as if I could see my wife wagging her finger at me in my mind.

That same moment my wife came in with the guy's wife and once again I congratulated myself on holding my tongue.

"He was just telling me the little baby was sick recently," I said to my wife.

"He is so cute. What happened?" my wife asked.

I had to admire my wife for following a rule she had tried unsuccessfully to teach me for years: compliment first.

The wife was the one who answered this time.

"He was running a temperature, so we thought we should just give him a cold shower and let him rest and he would be okay the next day. But the next day his temperature was worse, so we decided to take him to the hospital. We had to wait a long time before the doctor would see us. The doctor asked if we had his shot records and we said that we didn't. From that moment on everything changed. They said they were going to admit him and that he would be placed under observation for a virus."

She named a deadly virus I had heard of on the news. It had a name that was a combination of numbers and letters, but I had not paid much attention to it because according to what I heard in the news only little kids were vulnerable to it, and since I had no kids and was not a kid myself I paid no further attention.

"So they offered no treatment?" my wife asked.

"Just the occasional pain reliever," the alien wife said.

"Oh, dear," said my wife, apparently outraged.

"We were in that hospital for two days and my boy was not getting any better—in fact he was looking frail with each passing day. So one night I told my husband that we would leave the hospital the next morning and look for help for our son elsewhere. My husband agreed with me. The next morning when the doctor came in, we told him that we were going to leave. He was angry. He said we would be putting our child's life in danger and that this was a country of laws and that if anything happened to the baby we would be held responsible. We told him that we knew that already. At that point he said we should wait, that he wanted one of his colleagues to take a look at our boy. The colleague soon came. She was a foreigner. She smiled and picked up our boy and touched his cheeks and watched him wince. She flashed a light into his ears and said that he had an ear infection. She set up an antibiotic drip for him. Within an hour our boy was sitting up on the hospital bed and asking for food. By evening he was well enough for us to leave the hospital," she said.

"That was ridiculous," my wife said.

"We are just grateful that we still have our boy," the husband said.

I asked the wife if I could carry the baby. She nodded and handed the baby to me.

"I have never seen you carry a baby before," my wife said, breaking into a smile.

"There's a first time for everything," I said.

The husband nodded in agreement. The baby looked at me.

I wondered if I was going to say something wrong. I was going to offer the baby something to eat but I didn't know what the baby liked to eat; they were aliens, after all, and he was still frail from his illness.

I turned to my wife. She was looking at me in a way I have never seen her look at me before. Her eyes were filled with tenderness so heavy you couldn't cut it with a knife. I realized that there was nothing I would say at that moment that would be wrong and I began to rock the baby from side to side.

Feast

Everybody looked good on Alien Feast Day. It is said that even the sick became well on Alien Feast Day. Even if they were still feeling a little unwell, it was kind of hard to know because everyone came out gaily dressed.

Little children stood listlessly in groups acting the way children are wont to act all over the world. Becoming interested in one thing then losing interest very quickly and moving on to something else. The older kids who had witnessed the festival a few times in the past tried to act like they knew it all. They strutted around. Impatient to see things begin like everyone else then acting blasé like they had seen it all the very next minute. Then they grew curious all over again, asking questions and growing petulant when their parents seemed distracted and didn't respond quickly.

"What color of alien was it going to be this time?"

"If the aliens were so happy how come they didn't smile?"

"Why did they do it anyway?"

"Why aliens? Why not real people like the rest of us?"

"Was it true that the aliens got to eat whatever they chose before it was done?"

"Was it also true that in the past an alien had asked for something that was not available here and they had to go over the hills and valleys and through many mountains and rivers until they finally got the delicacy he had requested and then they brought it for him and after he ate then the deed was done?"

"Was it ever going to stop?"

Shhhh. Hush. You ask too many questions, the Elders said to the little ones. Who have questions ever helped in this world, they asked? Even as they answered the children's questions with a question of their own.

Turning once again to the children, they told them to just watch and observe the proceedings. That was how the Elders had learned the rules. That is how the children were going to learn, if only they could settle down and watch.

The children watched, observed, and grew quiet for a little while then like the restless little weaverbirds that they were, they began to ask questions again.

"What color of hood was it going to be this time?"

"Would it be a black, white, red, or purple hood?"

"All the rumors at school saying that the alien would not be hooded anymore? Why was a hood even necessary? Was there anything that was being hidden from their eyes? Even if they saw the proceedings with unhooded eyes what difference was it going to make at the end of the day when all is said and all is done?"

Asking questions to which no answers were obviously forthcoming becomes boring after some time, especially for young children who do not have the patience of philosophers.

So they began to do that other thing that children like to do even as the adults began to go about the business of the day. The adults were adept at this for they were not learning the ropes—they had done this deed many times and had become adept at what was going to be done.

So the children began to play their games.

They played *Boju Boju,* a game of hide-and-seek. They all went into hiding while the Seeker ran around saying *boju boju?* and looking for the luckless victim to catch who then becomes the next Seeker.

They played There Is Fire On the Mountain Run Run Run. They ran in every direction screaming about the fire on the mountain and asking everyone to run, run, run.

They played *Tinko Tinko*. The sound of their little hands growing surprisingly loud as they slammed against each other.

They played Who Is In The Garden?

They played the favorite game of the boys: Police and Thief. Some played the good guys while some played the bad guys. They searched furiously for the missing item until it was found.

And the girls got tired of playing with the boys and began to yell, "Girls and girls play together." And the boys too who were already tired of playing with the girls but didn't want to be the first to complain also began screaming, "Boys and boys play together!"

And the girls went off on their own to play their own game of Ten-Ten.

And the boys found a piece of brown rope and began to play Tug of War. They stretched their little muscles as they pulled and the losing side derived a lot of pleasure as they fell on the ground screaming the word *yakata*.

Soon they all decided that they'd have more fun by playing together and they gathered again both boys and girls and began to recite a poem about two blackbirds sitting on a tree, two blackbirds that had the odd names of Peter and Paul and how Peter soon flew away and then Paul seeing that Peter had flown away also decided to fly away and then there were no more blackbirds sitting on the tree.

All that playing had made them hungry and now their mind was on the food that they were going to eat after the hanging. The entire event was really about the feasting after all. So once again they returned to the subject of food.

Like the well brought-up kids that they were, they began to talk politely about the food that the alien was allowed to eat before the hanging.

"So if the alien wants a cake as big as a house, they'd order the cake?"

"Was it true that even if they wanted a big tub of ice cream they could get it?"

"Was it true that the alien could order any kind of sweet, toffee, candy, gum, that they wanted and it would be given to them?"

The answer to all their questions was of course *yes*. Just before the hanging the alien could request for any kind of food or drink. Any quantity and it would be provided.

They still found it somewhat difficult to wrap their heads around this fact. That it was even remotely possible to request for a food or drink or a type of candy and it would be provided with no questions asked. These children lived in a world where it seemed like they were always asking for things and in this world it was always the job of the adults to say no to their requests. Perhaps, the fate of the alien was not a bad one, really when you thought about it.

And the phrase *it wasn't so bad* rang like a song that played over and over again in their young heads.

It wasn't so bad . . . it wasn't so bad . . . it wasn't so bad . . .

"The day is far spent," the Announcer said.

It was funny how the Announcer came up with new expressions every year. Was there a little book he consulted from which he pulled out the expressions?

"We must begin to do what we have gathered to do," said the Announcer.

This too was a new expression. In the past he had used words like:

"Now the hour has come."

"It is that time of the year once again."

"OK, let's do it."

"And now, let us do as we have always done."

They brought out the alien. The alien's face was not covered. The aliens had the option of having their faces hooded or not.

According to the Elders this idea of deciding whether to have their face covered or not was yet another proof of how much choice the alien had in the matter.

Once again the Announcer cleared his throat and intoned:

"Accept our little sacrifice which we offer up on to you."

The alien was led to the stage. The rope was fastened around the alien's neck. The lever was pulled. The neck snapped. The alien was dead.

It was the children that started the race to the Feasting Hall where the food was already prepared and waiting. Soon they were joined by the adults.

They fell on the food and feasted with both hands. It was one day when they could eat as much as they wanted and even more. There was nothing wrong with stray pieces of food falling on the floor or drinks spilling from cups that were running over. It was allowed. That was even the point of the feast.

And that night, everyone slept soundly because on Alien Feast days everyone slept uncommonly well.

Some said it was the food.

Some said it was the drink.

Some said it was the salubrious weather.

Some said it was a sign that the alien sacrifice had been an acceptable one.

What no one could argue about was that after the hanging of an alien everyone always slept soundly. And the only

sound that could be heard all through the night was the
relentless musical song of deep snores.

Mark

When I was young there were three things my grand-mother loved to do: sunbathe, smoke her tobacco pipe, and tell me stories about the Red Planet.

"Make me my pipe and I will tell you a story about the Red Planet. My eyes are beginning to dim and I don't want to spill the tobacco all over myself," she'd say to me.

I would make her the pipe. I packed the aromatic to-bacco tightly into the pipe the way she preferred it. She did not like to light her pipe with safety matches, so I had to go to the kitchen and scoop burning pieces of charcoal with her metal gong the way she taught me to do it. She would nimbly pick up the coal with thumb and forefinger without a wince and drop it into her pipe. She would draw the pipe and slowly let the smoke through her nostrils. Her craggy face soon became relaxed and only then would she start telling me one of her stories.

"When the earth was still very young," she would begin.

"How do you mean young, Grandma?"

"So young one had to walk slowly and gingerly like a chameleon otherwise the earth would cave in."

"The earth was that young?" I asked.

"Yes, so young you did not need a hoe to dig the soil. You simply scooped up the dark earth with your hands be-fore planting your crops."

I placed my foot on the earth and pressed. It felt firm.

"That must be a really long time ago, Grandma," I said.

"Long to you, but not so long ago to me. Anyway, you must let me continue with my story or I will forget what story it was I was going to tell you," Grandma said.

"I am listening, Grandma," I said.

"Many years ago, the sky of the Red Planet hung over the earth like a low-hanging fruit. And here was the best part—the Red Planet was totally edible. You could cut and eat a piece of the Red Planet for food. The amazing thing was that it tasted so good. The reason why it tasted so good was because the piece that you cut transformed into whatever you desired to eat. So if your craving was for yam pottage you simply cut a piece of the overhanging Red Planet and it tasted like the best yam pottage you ever had.

"The inhabitants of the Red Planet did not mind people cutting and eating their planet as food because no sooner did you cut a piece than it grew right back. But there was one simple rule: one must cut and eat only the quantity that was enough to fill them. If you cut a bigger piece than would fill you, the Red Planet became angry and moved further away from the earth.

"For a long time everyone obeyed this rule and there was no problem. But as the earth began to get older and the number of people continued to grow, people began to worry if the Red Planet would still be there when they woke up the next morning. So what did they do? They began to cut more of the Red Planet than they could eat. But a sad thing was also happening. The piece they hoarded grew wormy and inedible. And another thing began to happen: the Red Planet began a fast dialogue with its legs and began receding further and further.

"One day the people of earth woke up and the Red Planet was gone. Gone to where man could neither reach it nor cut it to eat. That was how the Red Planet ran away from us. It ran so far away and did not look back."

Grandma paused and closed her eyes. She was silent. The only sound was the sound of her cold pipe as she moved it from one side of her mouth to the other. Her eyes were closed.

"Are you sleeping, Grandma?" I asked.

"Sleep? What am I doing with sleep? I will die soon and sleep forever, so what is the rush? Make me a fresh pipe," she said.

"But Father says you should smoke only a few pipes a day because of your health, Grandma," I said.

"And when did your father start caring so much about my health? Did he worry about my health when he nearly tore me in half when I was giving birth to him? I never smoke more than my body needs, and besides, tobacco is not planning to run away," Grandma said. "Make me a fresh pipe and I will tell you a story about the most beautiful girl on earth and how she ended up marrying a very ugly man from the Red Planet."

"The most beautiful girl, you said, Grandma?" I asked.

"I see that I have your attention now. You are just like your father," Grandma said.

I prepared a fresh pipe for her.

"So back when the earth was still young there once lived this girl who was so beautiful that her beauty could only be compared to the radiant sun and the ocean and to beautiful flowers. She was nicknamed Enenebejolu, meaning entrancing beauty that made one forget to go to the farm. She loved her nickname. She was not bashful, not one little bit. Soon enough everyone forgot her real name and began calling her only by her nickname, Enenebejolu.

"And then it was time for her to marry. Men from far and near began to ask for her hand in marriage. But for each suitor that came to propose she had a reason why she could not marry them.

"'Go away, you are too short,' she said to the short one.

"'You want to marry me, you who is as tall as a palm tree.'

"'You want to marry me? You are too dark-skinned. How will I see you when it is dark?'

"'No way can I marry you. Your skin is too fair. Are you a woman that you should be this fair-skinned? Please leave me alone. Must you get married? If you must marry why not look for your own kind?'

"A suitor with long hair she turned down by calling him bushy-haired.

"The hairless suitor she hissed at and sent away because he had no hair. 'How can I marry a bald-headed man when I am not a vulture?' she asked.

"No suitor was good enough for her.

"To the poor suitor she said, 'I can't marry you. You want me to leave my father's house to go and suffer in your house? No way am I doing that.'

"To the rich suitor she said, 'Oh no, not you. You want people to say I married you because of your wealth. No way. I want a husband I can work with so we can both grow rich together.'

"And soon Enenebejolu's news reached the Red Planet. You know how news travels fast even to the most distant planets. Now, you may not know this but the Red Planet has the ugliest men in the universe. The men from the Red Planet are rather harsh on the eyes. When news reached them that there was a beautiful girl down here who was turning down all the men who asked for her hand in marriage, they decided to send one of their own people to try. Now, don't forget that I had mentioned earlier that the men of the Red

Planet were ugly, but one thing they had in abundance was resourcefulness. So they came up with a plan. They each decided that they would contribute the most attractive part of their body to the man from their planet who was coming to ask Enenebejolu for marriage. One contributed his straight legs, another an impressive nose, and the other contributed his gleaming set of teeth.

"On the market day, the man from the Red Planet came into town. As soon as Enenebejolu set her eyes on him she fell in love with him. Before the man from the Red Planet could open his mouth to ask for her hand, she agreed to marry him. And that same day she agreed to follow him back to his planet. As they entered the Red Planet, her new husband began to return all the body parts he had borrowed to their original owners. Soon he had returned them all and he stood before Enenebejolu squat and ugly, and right before Enenebejolu's eyes was the ugliest creature she had ever seen. She realized her folly and she began to shed tears. First her eyes shed water, then they shed blood. That was how sad she was. To worsen matters, nobody in the entire Red Planet called her by her nickname."

Grandma rose and stretched.

"You have heard enough stories for one day. It is time for me to go inside," she said.

And then Grandma didn't come out of her room. I went to her room when I came back from school and I found her sitting on her *palaver* chair. She was wearing her olive-green sweater and her black beanie cap.

"Make me some tea," she said.

I poured the tea leaves into her black whistling kettle and added water. When the water with the tea leaves came to a boil, I took it off the stove and let the tea build some body, then I placed a tea-strainer on her large green metal cup and poured out the pitch-black tea. I gave her the cup, she pursed her lips and blew the top and took a little sip.

"Drink, Grandma. Tea is good for you. Soon you'd be strong again," I said.

I went to turn off the stove, but Grandma told me to turn it down low, but to leave it on. I could see that she was cold even though it was quite warm and I was sweating.

"All my friends and age-mates already left. They are calling me to come with them on a journey," she said

"What journey, Grandma? Can I come with you?" I asked.

"Heaven forbid that you will come with me," she said. "The journey is far and I am not quite ready. Traveling to a distant place requires preparation," she said.

The next day I went with Grandma to the forest to get some herbs from the *Ebenebe* tree for her fever. The tree stood alone in the forest as if other trees were scared to come too close to it. The tree had a white bark.

Grandma leaned on the tree and began to speak to it.

"O, highly respected one, we come to you to take of you to heal our body. Cutting into you is like cutting into our own skin, but we do it to make us better. We revere you and love you and will never hurt you. Give us your healing power, dearly venerated one. May we be healed of whatever ails us the way your bark heals after we cut you for our needs."

And then she gestured to me to cut and I did.

When we got back home Grandma emptied the bark into her pot and added water and placed it on the stove. Her stove was the old-fashioned type that needed to be pumped. I pumped the stove hard and soon the flame turned from orange to blue. The pot began to boil and the herbal aroma of the bark filled the room. I turned down the stove at Grandma's instruction and she removed the cover of the pot and moved her palaver seat so she was sitting directly beside the pot. She placed the pot between her legs and draped her blanket around herself so she was completely covered and began to breathe in the hot aromatic fumes from the boiled bark.

When she removed the blanket she was covered in sweat. She smiled.

"It is broken. I feel better," she said. "Come back tomorrow and I will tell you another story."

The next day Grandma was back in her usual place sitting in the sun.

"So where did I stop?" Grandma asked.

"You said you were going to tell me a new story," I said.

"I did? I wonder why I said that because I don't recall finishing the last story that I was telling you about the beautiful girl who married an ugly man from the Red Planet."

"I thought you did, Grandma."

"I didn't," Grandma said.

She leaned back on her chair and cleared her throat. She got her pipe going.

"So she began to live her new life with her new husband on the Red Planet. But to be honest she absolutely hated her new life. Remember, there was nobody to call her by her nickname, Enenebejolu. She worked from morning to night breaking rocks. First she attacked the hard red rocks with a little hammer and when a chunk fell off she had to break the chunk into little pieces. But why the breaking of rocks, you ask? Because that was what they ate on the Red Planet. They ate rocks for breakfast, lunch, and dinner. Some have speculated that it may be the reason why they had such hard faces. She had to cook the rocks too, and you know how long it takes for rocks to be cooked.

"Then one day she decided she had had enough and she decided to flee. She ran and she ran. Her husband gave chase. I told you how far the Red Planet was from our own, but she ran without looking back. And her husband ran after her without stopping.

"Just when she thought she would fall down and die from exhaustion, she glimpsed the line that separated the Red Planet from ours. As she went to cross the line her husband tried to grab her but she was too fast for him. Unfortunately his long nails made a groove on her back in the area between her shoulder blades. This is the reason why there is a line that runs the length of our backs.

"Now you must go, I need to gather my strength," Grandma said.

Towards the end of that year, I left for boarding school. When I returned, my grandma had left for the journey that she always talked about. The news was hidden from me because my parents were worried that it would affect my academic performance.

It has been many years since Grandma told me the stories about the Red Planet, but today I looked up at the sky over New England and the sky is red, mostly scarlet. It looks almost as if I could touch it if I tried. The color calls out to me, reminding me of my grandmother and her stories about the Red Planet.

Spaceship

I must have been about ten or eleven when an alien spaceship landed in our village. Clearly written on the side was *Tatuala*. We would spend months trying to crack the meaning of the word just as we had tried years ago to decode the meaning of the Latin expression *Domini Opera* written on the tailboard of a passing mammy wagon.

The alien who emerged from the spaceship did not appear much different from us. The only thing about him was that though dressed in a military uniform, he looked quite short. The village Elders remarked that he would probably not qualify to be a soldier here in our country on account of his height. And one other minor thing was that he walked with both feet at once. Otherwise, in every other aspect, he acted like a man whose vehicle had broken down in a place where he did not know anyone.

As was the usual practice with anything that was unusual, the village Elders gathered to find out what he wanted. He explained that he was actually on his way to another planet when his spaceship began to lose velocity and he was forced to land in our village. How exactly did they converse? In what language did they speak to one another? The Elders would later tell us that though the alien had only moved his lips slightly, they could understand everything he said. He had somehow communicated his words clearly into their heads. His only request was that he be granted permission to leave his spaceship in our village while he traveled back to his home planet to get the parts he needed to repair his broken-down spaceship. This was not an onerous request in any way. The Elders agreed. He signaled to his planet with a small pinging device that looked like a Walkie-Talkie and they sent another spacecraft to come and ferry him back. The spacecraft that took him back did not land on our village soil. It hovered above the ground and our swarthy alien guest jumped in and the spacecraft took off.

The Elders told the young people in the village to treat the spaceship with respect the same way we had been told to respect the first billboard mounted in the village square that advertised Peak Evaporated Milk.

If the alien had come back after a few days to repair his spaceship and return back to his planet there would have been no story to tell. But a week passed and the alien did not return.

Villagers began to comment on the spaceship that was green in color and shaped like a terrapin's carapace.

"It looks so solid and heavy yet it can fly really fast. Look how it glided noiselessly through the air, and when it landed it came to a halt without a single sound. The airplanes that pass through here make so much noise even though they are so far up in the sky. This one did not even make a single sound," one villager said.

"Great things don't make noise. It is only empty things that call attention to themselves by screaming aloud to everyone, *look at me, look at me, why are you ignoring me?* But solid things, ah, they never shout. Look, let me tell you, it is only rickety and ramshackle motor vehicles that you can hear their sounds from a mile away. The really good cars you won't even know they are coming and then suddenly they are behind you. Thank goodness for their horns; otherwise they'd knock one down," another Elder said, further reinforcing the fact that the broken-down spaceship was not like the proverbial empty vessel that reputedly made a lot of noise.

"You know what the he-goat said is quite true. According to the he-goat it is important to move around and not stay in one place; otherwise you'll think that there is only one kind of leaf that is edible," said another. "If we had not seen this one, how would we know that the airplane that flies past our village sky is not the only thing made out of metal that flies?"

Everyone in the village agreed that indeed the spaceship was a thing of wonder and that it was the most amazing thing that flew in the skies.

Matters would have ended just like they did regarding the billboard, which was soon obscured by tall weeds and was soon forgotten after a couple of weeks. But a few things happened that made people begin to talk more about the spaceship.

For the first time in the history of the village, the village elementary school St Matthews came first in the School District Bands and March Past competition. This was an unbelievable accomplishment considering that the school competed against students from the other schools like St Martin de Porres and Maria Goretti—schools from much bigger towns. Bigger towns had electricity and electric irons and bleach and starch and shoe polish all of which counted for much and could make a difference when it came to appearance. Bigger town schools also had more impressive musical instruments. Despite the fact that the students from our elementary school used charcoal irons to iron their uniforms, the judges said they were the best school at the march past. They said that our pupils were particularly impressive during the march past when they were commanded to turn their eyes right even as they kept on goose-stepping.

A week later the school's relay team came first in the District Schools' Athletics Competition. This again had never happened. Nothing close to it, even. There was no doubt that something was going on. Something had happened to the village water source or to the air that we breathed. The puzzle was soon solved. We had almost forgotten about the spaceship. But how could we have forgotten about it? Yes, it was the spaceship that had brought about our winning the competitions. Surely, the spaceship was a benevolent god of some sort; otherwise how could all these good things that have never been witnessed in the history of our village only begin to happen now that the strange vehicle was docked in our village?

The Elders, who had an explanation for everything, had an explanation for this one.

"Remember that time we had darkness in the afternoon that we were later told on the radio that it was something called an eclipse? Remember all the misfortune that followed in its wake? The poor harvest that year and how all the fish moved downstream and there were only scrawny crabs left in the river? And all that was because of the eclipse. No surprise that what has been happening is because of the spaceship. Every strange and new thing brings along with it something good or something bad," said one of the Elders.

Elders have a long memory and they love to tell stories, so soon one story followed another. There was the year this other thing happened and there was a great change that happened that year and it was only after that people realized that there had been a link between what happened then and what followed . . .

The thing that nobody could explain though, was why it was taking the alien in the military uniform who had promised to be back to fix his broken-down spaceship that long to return for his space vehicle.

There was one more thing that happened after the spaceship docked in our village. Bell of Hope, the trader who owned the village store, bought a pickup truck. In a village where the ownership of a Raleigh bicycle was a major life achievement and where people aspired to ownership of the much revered Honda Benly motorcycle—the purchase of a pickup truck was like someone buying an airplane in the larger world.

Again, this was no mere occurrence and could not have happened without some causative agent.

Whose idea was it to begin making sacrifices to the alien ship? No one was sure, but it was probably the Elders.

We woke up one day and there were bottles of Fanta and Coke and shiny pennies and a couple of woven white fabrics right by the spaceship. Someone or some people had decided to make sacrifices to the spaceship.

The people who made the sacrifices promised to offer more things to the spaceship as their fortunes improved.

"If our village has received all the blessings we received recently even without giving anything in return you can imagine what is going to happen if we show our appreciation by offering a little sacrifice?"

Some people argued against the idea of sacrificial offering to the spaceship.

"Before you offer something to an idol, that god or idol must have a priest. The priest is the spokesperson of the god among us men. It is the priest that will now tell you what the god likes to eat and what is forbidden to the god. If you give gin to a goddess that drinks only Fanta,

you would end up offending the god and there'd be consequences," someone said.

"This one is not like the gods we know. What we need
to do is what we have done. This god is from a different
world. Let it choose what it likes to eat from what we have
offered," one of those who made the sacrifice said.

And that was where the argument ended. Nothing more
was said because there was no noticeable improvement in
the lives of those who made the sacrificial offerings.

But that was not the end of the matter. One day Keke,
who had suffered migraines since birth, did something
rather strange. He went to the spaceship with a bowl of water and rinsed off some part of the spaceship into the bowl
and drank. The day after he drank, he told his neighbors
that his migraine had subsided. He said it was not completely gone but that he had only done it once and he was
sure if he did it many more times and even washed his face
with the water, the migraine would disappear completely.

No one tried to stop Keke or argue with him. His migraines had become every villager's headache over the years
and anything that made him feel better was a welcome relief.

A fence made out of red rope and wood was found around
the spaceship one morning. It was not a sturdy fence in any
way but more like a demarcation tool. Again, it was the Elders who had made the decision to have the fence around
the spaceship. They said it was not anything out of the ordinary, but a way to show a little reverence for *the Visitor*—
for that was the euphemism for the spaceship these days.

At about this time people began to say that they observed some things about the spaceship.

Some said that it glowed in the inky blackness of the
night when there was no moon. That its glow was faint like
the low-watt glow of ancient fireflies.

Some said they heard a gentle hum from the ship when all was quiet at night and even the night insects had gone silent and fallen asleep.

Some said they heard movements within the insides of the ship like the gentle near-quiet light footsteps of the chameleon.

Some said there was a strange smell in the air of the village that seemed to emanate from the ship. It was a smell that was different depending on the person describing it. Some said it smelled like the after-smell of burning grass.

Some said they had heard and felt the earth around the village shrug mildly and tremble on a few occasions. That it wasn't anything major, but it was like the earth shrugged slightly. But because these phenomena had no negative effect on anyone, they were waved off as nothing significant.

One mid-afternoon a commercial vehicle pulled up at the village square and a man emerged asking for the way to his father's compound. This in itself was unheard of in the history of our village. It was even stranger than the arrival of the spaceship. How is it possible for a man not to know the way to his father's compound? Was that not where he was born? Where his umbilical cord was buried? Where he emerged from to go to the farm and the stream?

The man turned out to be Robert. Robert had set an academic record in the village elementary school that was unequaled to date. He had gone on to set a record in the secondary school as well. The villagers had pulled their resources together to send him to Fourah Bay College in Sierra Leone. It was expected that he would in return come back and sponsor other children from the village for further education. But Robert never came back after his college education. There had been many letters and telegrams sent to him to remind him to return, but he did not respond to any. Now Robert was back.

There was great rejoicing at Robert's return. He said he was going to build a community secondary school and serve as the principal. This was great news.

The big question remained why he had chosen to come back at this time. Robert said that it was as if a force was pulling him. He said he felt like a fish that was being reeled in by unseen hands. He said the best way to describe how he felt was how iron-filings found it impossible to resist the lure of a magnet.

Ah, the Elders said. What other force could have pulled him home if not our visitor—the spaceship?

There was now some anxiety about what would happen if the alien came back to take his ship. What would happen after the visitor leaves? Would our good fortune dry out like a lake that had its source cut off? What can we do to detain the spaceship further or even make it stay with us permanently?

One of the Elders said that we should treat the spaceship the way we would treat a visitor that we did not want to leave.

How exactly do you do that, someone asked?

The familiar scenarios known to everyone in the village are the strategies for sending away a visitor that was overstaying their welcome. You could yawn and say "oh by this time last night we were already asleep in bed" or you could get a broom and start sweeping and they'd take the hint.

Besides, the spaceship, even though it was euphemistically referred to as the Visitor, could not be treated like a human visitor. A human visitor could be offered food and drinks and made to feel at home. They could even be offered the most comfortable bed in the house. But how do you detain a spaceship?

Some people had made sacrifices to it but there was no sign that they were favored above those that did not. Someone else remarked that sacrificing the wrong thing to a deity might attract wrath instead of blessings.

We woke up to the smell of smoke. The village sky was covered with smoke. When we looked up we saw that the smoke was coming from the farmlands that lay about three miles from the village. Everyone began to run towards the farmlands. When they reached the farmlands they discovered that overnight a fire had burned through the farmlands destroying the corn, yam, cassava, and sweet potatoes that were the staple of the community. There was nothing left as all the farms lay next to each other.

Wailing rose up in the sky like the smoke from the burning farmland. What were people going to feed on? What would they sell to make money to buy the items they did not grow? Almost everyone in the village depended on the crops from their farms to live.

What has brought this upon us, the villagers asked?

What have we done wrong that we should have the very food taken from our mouths?

Who have we wronged that we are surely to die from starvation?

What other trade can we pursue now that our crops have perished?

No one asked what had started the fire or where the fire came from. In the village, all misfortunes were viewed as one and their external manifestations were not considered as important as their root cause.

The night after the fire that burned the farms it began to rain. The rain fell in gigantic pellets vehemently and relentlessly and did not pause to draw breath. It rained like that for two days without ceasing. People could not leave their homes for fear that they'd be swept away by the flood.

Just as the rain had started without thunder clouds, it stopped abruptly and the sun came out as if it had not gone anywhere. As the sun emerged, so did the Elders.

"We were young once, and now we are old, but we have never seen anything like this since our ancestors founded this village. First, it was fire, then water. Each of the elements is enough to kill," the Elders said.

And then all the Elders arrived at the same thought all at once.

It must be the spaceship.

It must be the strange visitor.

First it lured us close with the empty gift of good fortune before unleashing its peril upon us.

It was decided by the Elders that the spaceship must go.

But how to do this?

There was no way of sending an emissary to the planet from which it came to come and carry their thing.

To make telephone calls to the city, the villagers had to go to the post office. But how do you place a call to the alien when he has not bothered to leave a forwarding address nor a contact number behind?

Even if a young man in the village volunteered to go, how would he prepare for the journey? How much food would he pack and how many gallons of water would be enough to take along for the trip? What was the distance between the planet from which the spaceship came and our village?

It was decided by the Elders to do to the spaceship what was usually done to recalcitrant gods—the villagers would ignore it and turn their backs to it. They would live their lives as if it didn't exist.

And that was what they did.

Soon, grasses and creeping vines and thistles and wild shrubs began to sprout around the spaceship. The soil around the village was fertile. Soon the spaceship was covered with wild vegetation.

Sometimes when there was a strange noise at night we would say to ourselves it must be the spaceship calling out to its owner, *Come and get me, come and get me,* why *have you turned your back at me?*

Sacrifice

This was the way it always happened. Every year an alien spaceship would quietly descend. Its doors gently swing open. A young man from our village would obediently walk into the spaceship. The spaceship door then glides forcefully closed. After which the spaceship departs.

This was our entire relationship with them ever since the days of our ancestors. It is the way we have always done it and the same way our children would do it. Those are the terms of the treaty that our ancestors signed with them. It says that every year we must give them a young man or they'd attack us and take all of us away and sow chemicals on our land so that nothing could ever grow on it again and poison our streams so that whosoever drank from it will burn up and die.

It sounded fair, to us. We had nothing with which we would have fought them. We were just ordinary folk. All we had were our machetes for farming, our single barrel guns for hunting, and our fishing nets and hooks. There was no way we were going to be able to fight them and their space-ships that glided through the air. They could wipe us out by the press of one button.

There were different stories about the young men and women who left on the spaceship.

Some said that they had gone to a better place, a place better than our lives of endless toil here in the village.

Others said that they'd train them to become Engineers

and Pilots and Scientists and they'd soon be piloting space-ships like the aliens.

To some they have gone to a place where all the comforts can be summoned by the touch of a button. Over there they have robots that bring them cups of water and serve them tea, some said.

A few said that they were better off there. Over there they didn't even have to lift a finger, was some people's opinion.

Some people said that when they got to the place the spaceships came from, they were given beautiful women as wives and their only assignment was to reproduce with the women so they could bring forth a superior race of beings that were indestructible.

The more cynical types said that they were etherized in space labs while their bodies were examined under microscopes. That they stared all day with sightless eyes like fishes preserved in chloroform in a Biology laboratory.

Some of the other comments were too fantastic to believe if not downright cruel. They said that the young men and women were sacrificed on a piece of rock that was shaped like the spaceship the moment they got to the other place.

In spite of the different opinions, there was one thing that everyone was sure about and upon which there was no argument. Those who left never came back. Not a single one of them ever came back and nothing was heard of them again.

The truth is that we had peace. We could farm and harvest our crops and sit under the moon at night to share stories. We told ourselves that it could have been worse.

What if we had gone to war with the Aliens and they had defeated us? Would we have not ended up losing our young men and women in the war?

What if they had defeated us and decided to carry us

away into captivity to their strange land? What would we have done? To be held captive here on earth was bad, now compare that to being held captive in a strange planet where it was rumored the sun never stopped shining.

If we have ninety-nine gods in our village, the woman Makodi must have visited the shrine of each single one of them to ask for a child. She had married two husbands before her present one and was sent packing on each occasion because of her barrenness. It was when she married her third husband that she finally became pregnant and had her son Obiajulu. Everyone in the village was aware that Makodi treated Obiajulu like an egg. He was the kid whose mother dressed him up in a thick sweater simply because the sky was gray. He was that kid whose mother stood by the edge of the village soccer pitch carrying a gallon of water and hopping from one leg to the other waiting and hoping her son did not get tackled and fall. If he did fall she would be the one to quickly rush into the field to ask him if he was hurt. Their relationship had become the stuff of legend so much so that doting kids told their moms to let them be that they were not like Obiajulu. She was there waiting for him at the close of school. At first his classmates teased him, but they soon got tired because his mother always found a way to top her last act of embarrassment.

It came to a point that it was not possible to talk about Obiajulu without mentioning his mother.

If only she could have another child so she could stop suffocating this one with this type of excessive love that kills, some said.

She may never let him out of her sight long enough to get married, others said.

Ah, this life. Some children are praying for their mothers to look their way, this one must be praying for his mother to look away if even for one minute. All that love and attention must be suffocating. This was from another woman who lived down the same street.

There were a few other more philosophical and empathetic comments as well. These few voices commented on how long it had taken her to finally have a child of her own.

Why should we blame her? First time no luck. Second time no luck, only frustration and then sent away empty-handed, and then finally the third time she got this boy. What do you expect? We must learn from the mother-hen even though we think we are wiser than chickens, but look at the way the mother-hen guards and guides her eggs and her little chicks.

You know what they say: If you have children, worrying about them would nearly do you in, and if you don't have children, worrying about having children would nearly kill you. So either way children mean anxiety and worry.

For a boy who was so doted on, Obiajulu was quite a good boy. Always happy to run occasional errands for his mom and quite a good sport when he was playing soccer with his friends.

He hardly ever got into fights with any of his playmates, but he was not boring because he equally had an impish sense of mischief and a surprisingly sharp tongue that could spit out biting words when the need arose.

This combination made Obiajulu well liked though his friends would always end whatever they asked him to do with the expression "if your mother lets you."

Finding a palm frond by the doorsteps of your house in the village meant that the house would produce the next person that would be put on the Alien ship. It is quite possible that in the early days people cried and screamed in protest when they saw the palm frond by their door-steps but that must have been in the past. People simply accepted it and basically saw it as their own way of building the community.

So when Makodi woke up and saw a palm frond by her doorstep and started screaming everyone in the village was startled but not surprised.

"Who owns the evil hand that wants to snatch my only palm nut that I got after many fruitless years of wandering in the bush with empty hands?" she screamed as she began running through the length and breadth of the village.

"Many people have four, five, six, and seven. I have just the one. Many have more than enough to spare and what does Makodi own? I have no bundles of damask like other women. I do not own a big house. The only piece of cloth that I own that should warm me on cold nights is what you want to take away from me."

Some in the village considered what Makodi was doing bad form. It was really quite unusual for people to complain the way she was doing when they saw a palm frond by their doorsteps. They did complain but quite mutedly, usually in the privacy of their inner rooms behind closed doors.

"What exactly does she want? She wants the entire village to be wiped out for the sake of her son?"

"Is she the first or is she going to be the last?"

"It is not a bad thing for her to cry. We all cried in the past, but we cried silently and we did it indoors."

"Every life is important, whether the life of her son or the lives of all those who had gone in the past, but what matters most is our continued survival and existence as a people."

"As many have said in the past, who knows what the journey holds for him? He may like it even more up there than he does down here. If it was so bad out there I am sure many would have come back to tell us how badly they fared over there."

Whether Makodi heard any of their comments or not no one could tell. She was undeterred as she ran back and forth through the village cursing and screaming.

"What crime did my one and only son commit that you chose to punish him this way?" she asked.

To this comment many responded that it was quite possible to choose where one wanted to be buried, but who has ever heard of one choosing where they were to be born? What a luxury that would be if we had a hand in the matter, they said.

The day that the palm frond was left on Makodi's doorstep was unusually gray. It was not threatening to rain but it was just gloomily overcast.

But there were also those who believed that it was somewhat unfair to ask of Makodi her only son whom she had been blessed with after many years of fruitless toil.

"She is not young anymore and besides it was so hard for her to have that boy. It is sad. I can see why the thought of losing her boy will make her lose it completely," someone said.

"It is much easier for those of us with more than one child to bear to see one of them taken away but for her with just that one boy it must really be heartbreaking," another said.

"What is to be done? What can we do? This life is indeed unfair, but we must continue to manage it because there is just one world—this is the only world we have. What choice do we have than to continue to take the good with the bad," were the words of another sympathizer.

Every ear was keen to hear what the Elders were going to say. They were the ones who had reached the peace agreement with the Aliens. The Elders were the one who had received this tradition of doing things from those who had gone before. Surely they had something to say maybe they had a solution even.

The Elders were murmuring and mumbling so much so that one could hardly hear them. Usually the Elders spoke clearly and forcefully but this time it was different. Why were they not speaking clearly? Was there something they didn't want all ears to hear? When they began to speak clearly above the muffle they spoke in riddles and obscure parables.

"What type of pain would the body experience that would make the eyes shed blood instead of tears?" they asked.

"Is there anything we are seeing today that we have not seen before?"

"The only new thing that will happen on this earth is if the heavens decide to fall upon the earth and cover it all up," they said.

"One little fart can ruin a gathering."

"One bad apple spoils the whole . . ."

"A little leaven ferments the whole lot."

The Elders said this and they said that. They beat around the bush without bringing forth anything fruitful. People listened closely to hear what the way out was going to be.

Meanwhile, Makodi was still wailing through the entire village screaming herself hoarse.

"Is this how you people are going to be watching? Is no one going to come to my help?"

"What exactly does she want us to do?" many asked.

"But I thought you people loved my son Obiajulu. Obiajulu my son who plays with your children. You people always stop me to compliment me on how well behaved he is, are you all going to fold your hands and watch him go, just like that?"

"Why is she talking like she is the first and only person to have her son taken away? Have most of us not been through the same thing?"

"When a bird sees a piece of stone coming towards it, it flies away, it does not wait to be hit. When a goat sees an object coming its way to hit it, even the goat gets up and runs away. Do you people expect me to fold my hands as this thing is coming towards me?" she asked.

By now ears were growing weary from listening to Makodi. Even her voice was beginning to grow hoarse from all the crying and screaming she had been doing the entire day. It was getting to the time that the ship was going to arrive from space. Her son had refused to eat all day and had been sitting on the bed he still shared with his mother.

When Makodi realized that the time was drawing near for her son to be taken away she returned to her house and stopped crying. She told her son to take his bath after which she told him to have something to eat and then she dressed him up in his best clothes. She too went and had a bath and dressed up in her best clothes.

They both came out and sat on a wooden bench and began to wait for the arrival of the spaceship that was going to take her son away.

Now tongues began to wag and get busy at the sight of mother and child dressed in their best clothes waiting for the spaceship.

"Was she not the one crying only a few moments ago?"

"What exactly is she up to this time and why is she dressed like someone heading to a party? Does she want us to think all the tears were for nothing?"

"Why is the boy dressed so colorfully? Does she not know that as soon as he boards the ship they are going to give him new clothes because the kind of clothes we wear here are different from what they wear over there?"

Soon, the Alien spaceship arrived like it always did. It glided in gently and descended. Makodi walked towards the spaceship holding Obiajulu's hands. As Obiajulu started to climb the stairs into the spaceship Makodi climbed with him, not letting go of his hand.

"Where is she going? Has she gone mad? They only take sons not old women, or doesn't she know that?" someone asked.

"I will go with him. It is either we go together or he is not going," she said.

"Let go of his hands. He must go alone. Do not bring disaster upon us all," the Elders said.

Makodi would not listen but went into the spaceship with her son.

There was a little scuffle inside the ship. The door did not close.

An Alien's hand pushed Makodi and Obiajulu out of the spaceship. The door of the spaceship closed. The spaceship left empty.

The Elders were the first to start wailing. Other villagers soon joined in.

"What shall we do? Surely, they are coming back to attack us," they said.

Many eyes were turned to the sky waiting for the attack, but it never came. The alien spaceship did not return. Not that day. Not that year. Not even the year after that.

Light

One day while she was weeding her farm, a ray of blue light from the sky fell on Bukwu. After Bukwu saw the blue light she became a totally different person. She was tilling the soil when the blue light came down from outer space and enveloped her. She said the light had been so bright it was like every other thing around her was in darkness— though it happened in the afternoon—as the light zeroed in on her and she could feel its rays on even the littlest strand of hair on her neck. She said the effect of the light on her was refreshing—like dipping into a cool stream on a muggy day. The way she described the light—she did not use the word *alien*, neither did she say the light was from a different planet—she simply said that the light that fell on her *was not of this world*.

When she was questioned by the village Elders, she said that she had not heard any voices when the light enveloped her, but that she had felt a beautiful warm glow as if someone had poured something sweet all over her.

The question about hearing voices had been a trick question by the village Elders to actually confirm if she had lost her mind. As everyone in the village probably knew, to hear voices was to go mad. But nobody in their living memory had ever reported seeing a strobe of light descend directly on them from outer space.

Bukwu said that after the light had ascended she had seen a shiny piece of brown rock on the ground where the light had touched. This turned out to be a problem because, when the Elders of the village went back with her to where she said the incident had happened, there was no piece of rock of any color, shape, or size to be found. This made the village Elders raise their eyebrows skeptically, but they had not said a word and had instead nodded sagely as if they agreed with her.

It was not uncommon for people in the village to claim to see things. Some had even claimed to have seen ghosts in the past, but to say one had seen blue light descend from the sky on a person who was busy working in their farm was unheard of and deserved some attention.

Why Bukwu, of all people, was the most often repeatedly asked question.

Bukwu who was known to be the most quarrelsome person in the village? Was there a man, woman, or child that she had not had a quarrel with?

Everyone in the village knew it was time to go to bed when Bukwu served her husband dinner. She was the last person to finish preparing the evening meal and by the time she was done it was close to bedtime. Her husband would be sitting on his easy chair shaking his feet, nodding and hissing and fuming as she went about leisurely making the meal. When she was done cooking, she would serve him the food casually.

"Your food is here. You better eat quickly I need to go to sleep," she would add.

She did not bother to eat because she was in the habit of nibbling at whatever she wanted as she cooked, so by the time the meal was ready she was already full.

"Is this food my evening meal or my breakfast?" her husband would ask.

"Please eat so I can clear the plates and go and rest. Stop

asking me questions for which I have no answers."

As they argued their voices would rise. Everyone in the village would know that Bukwu and her husband were quarreling once again about her late preparation of his evening meal and they would get ready for bed because it meant the night was already far spent.

Her late night cooking and the subsequent quarrel that followed was the first thing to cease after Bukwu saw the blue light from space in the farm.

Surprised by this change, people began asking questions. They listened in vain every night to hear Bukwu's querulous voice scolding her husband, but all they heard from their compound was silence.

To questions from surprised villagers—for, as it is well known in the village, one person's business is everyone's business—why she had stopped her late night cooking and quarreling with her husband, Bukwu responded with a series of profound-sounding koans.

"Quarreling and fighting is not food. No amount of quarreling can fill the stomach," she said. At another time she responded with: "No dead person was ever eulogized on their dying day for being the most quarrelsome person who ever lived."

"Every couple has disagreements; it is those who bring theirs out in the open that the world laughs at," she told another inquirer.

Many in the village were lost for words about Bukwu's transformation. There had never been anything like it before. The closest thing to it was when the village drunkard's father gave him a haircut and dressed him in new clothes and found a wife for him. The drunkard had hibernated and acted sober for a couple of weeks and had then gone back to his old drinking and falling-down ways.

Bukwu was the leader of the *Npotompo* dancing group. They met every week to rehearse. It was a group made up of young women and men. Some of the men were still single. Ordinarily, single men dancing with married women was frowned on but a little less so if they were members of a dancing group. It definitely meant that at some point they would have to present their dance to entertain the entire community and this would suggest that there could be nothing clandestine about their dancing. Bukwu had quarreled with her husband over her membership of the dancing group and how on days when they met to rehearse she prepared dinner early to enable her to go on time.

After Bukwu saw the light she called her group together and told them that she no longer wished to be a part of the dancing group.

"My heart is no longer in it. I do not want to waste what is left of my life on earth dancing. I plan to do some more important things as long as I am still breathing," she said.

"Are you saying we are idle and that is why we dance? What has come over you? Is dancing not a way of taking a break from the stress and worries of day-to-day work?" they asked her.

"Nothing wrong with doing what your heart tells you is right," Bukwu said. "As for my own heart, it has told me different, and I will do exactly as it says," Bukwu added. She was not speaking in an angry tone. None of the women or men in the group would have dared engage the old Bukwu in an argument.

"But what is wrong with dancing?" they asked. "Even in one of the holy books a man danced so energetically until his clothes tore into two."

"Some things are not bad strictly speaking, the only problem is that there is no profit in them," Bukwu responded.

Even her new manner of speaking was somewhat strange. People did not speak that way to each other in the village. She was beginning to sound like an oracle.

"But you can at least watch us practice our dance. You have been a part of *Npotompo* since it started," they begged her.

"What one does not eat one must not use one's teeth to share for one's children to eat," she said and turned her back to them.

❖

The question that everyone in the village continued to ask was—where was the old Bukwu? Where had she gone? Where was she hiding? Who took her away and brought us this faded, fake, inauthentic replacement? Who took her away? Who took her away we are asking a second time? Who is this person that you have given to us that tastes bland like unsalted soup?

Bukwu was the only woman in the village that whistled. Not that whistling by women was forbidden, but it was frowned at. A woman whistling was viewed as somewhat wanton. Bukwu was famous for her ability with a kind of song known as *ikpe. Ikpe* was a song composed in the moment to mock your enemies. The only unwritten rule about *ikpe* was that you must never mention your enemy's name in the song. Bukwu's *ikpe* was usually hilarious and entertaining as she switched from singing it to whistling. People would often gather to listen to her even as they tried to decode which of her many enemies she was now mocking. But as soon as she saw the light, her singing and whistling stopped.

When she was asked she said it was better to have lots of friends than to have lots of enemies. And that was all she was going to say about the matter.

For the longest time, speculation had been rife about Bukwu's relationship with Lucky, the chief baker of the village bakery. Lucky was a bachelor. He was muscular, always smiling. He had a radio which he carried around on his shoulder all the time. Bukwu worked the night shift at the bakery. She was one of those who cleaned up the bread when it came out of the bakery and put them in a plastic wrap with a label and deposited the bread in dozens on a palette. It was considered a stroke of good fortune to have an alternative means of income in the village. On many occasions Bukwu had been seen emerging from Lucky's room with a cup of tea. When asked, she said that she had gone there to get herself a cup of tea to go with the free loaf of bread every bakery worker received when the bread was baked.

On another occasion she said she had gone to rest her feet after working through the night. When Lucky was asked, he laughed out loud the way he always did and said he had an open door policy and that everyone was welcome to come to his room.

After Bukwu saw the light, she resigned from her job at the bakery. Not that she put in a resignation formally; she simply stopped showing up at the bakery. She also stopped seeing Lucky.

Now that Bukwu had become a different person, what about Lucky?

Was Lucky going to stop laughing out loud as was his habit?

Was Lucky going to start closing his door?

Was the number of female slippers in front of Lucky's door going to be fewer in number?

Was Lucky going to stop cradling his radio on his chest with its volume cranked up high?

Lucky laughed out loud when he heard these questions.

He said that he was not the one who had *seen* something and that he was happy with his life the way it was and did not see the need to change.

What about Bukwu's long-suffering husband who was used to eating his dinner late at night?

Did he miss their frequent quarrels when Bukwu would curse him out and tell him to try and be a *real* man instead of an imitation?

Did he miss the old Bukwu whom he once described as a vehicle driving through a thicket pulling at shrubs and ropes and grasses?

When he was asked, he responded in the riddles and parables which also made everyone in the village remember the saying that a piece of soap wrapped in a leaf soon becomes one with the leaf.

He had said to those who asked that it was a difficult thing to adjust to having one's bath with cold water after years of using hot water, but that it was also interesting to discover that having a bath with cold water was not such an unpleasant experience after all.

He also said that it was a totally different experience for someone who once had a pet tiger to adjusting to living with a cat, but that one soon discovered that the tiger and the cat are both animals and had their uses.

For anyone familiar or unfamiliar with village life, the question now was what did Bukwu do with herself now that she was no longer the Bukwu we all used to know?

There is of course no need to ask what the old Bukwu did with herself. Or do we need to be reminded about all that the old Bukwu did. In that case here goes.

The old Bukwu cursed.

The old Bukwu fought.

The old Bukwu cursed her enemies in song and whistling.

The old Bukwu quarreled with her husband, cooked late dinners, and called him a poor excuse of a man.

The old Bukwu cursed her Maker every day and wondered why she had been brought into this miserable world only to suffer and to die without knowing what it was like to enjoy life.

The old Bukwu went to her farm to work. She tilled. She planted. She weeded. She harvested.

She told stories about other people and spread gossip around the village, which was why behind her back she was nicknamed Radio Without Battery.

The old Bukwu danced with men in her dancing group.

The old Bukwu was always seen going in and out of the room of the chief baker Lucky.

The old Bukwu talked even when she had nothing to say.

The old Bukwu moved around like a bolt of lightning. Never pausing except to strike.

What can we say about the new Bukwu?

She was everything that the Old Bukwu was not. You could hardly hear her footsteps when she walked.

She barely spoke above a whisper.

But she was still the worker that she was. If a woman's work is never done, a village woman's work was often never even started. Life in the village was difficult, and farming required labor and patience even though in return one got just enough to sustain oneself. She still went to the farm to plant and weed and hoe and harvest. The same kind of crops that had left her ancestors poor was still the same thing she planted. Corn, cassava, sweet potatoes, and yams. Crops that yielded little, but wrung a lot of sweat from the brows of those who planted them.

It would have been good to say that things around Bukwu's life began to change thereafter. For instance, that she became rich or found great fame and that her life began to shine in new ways. None of those things happened.

One day Bukwu woke up as if startled awake and began to murmur to herself.

It was her husband who was sleeping on a separate bed in the same room who first heard her. It must be mentioned that they had ceased to sleep as man and wife a long time ago and shared the same room as siblings would.

Bukwu was restless and quickly began to get ready in a hurry like someone who must get to somewhere fast.

"What is the matter?" her husband asked.

"I must go to the farm fast. My light is fading," Bukwu said.

Her husband who was already getting used to her strange ways tried to decode what she meant by this. It was not yet fully morning but he was sure the sun would soon be out.

"The light that touched me. Yes, that light. It is beginning to fade and I must not let it fade out. I must return to where it first touched me so that it can touch me again," Bukwu said.

From that day onwards Bukwu would wake up early to leave for the farm. To those who asked she would say that she was going to wait for the light to touch her once again.

She would usually leave for the farm at the same time every day and just as people had been able to tell that it was time to go to bed by way of her late dinners they could now tell that it was time to begin their day whenever Bukwu set out for the farm to wait for the light to fall on her, again.

Traveler

Mine wasn't the only empty seat on the train, so I wondered why he came to sit beside me. I was getting used to sitting alone on the train on this trip. Not that I minded. During a past trip a beautiful young female college student with a dazzling set of teeth once sat beside me. The train was full. We traveled in silence. Shortly thereafter at the next stop someone got down and I stood up to go and take the vacant seat. As I asked her to excuse me while I passed, she smiled at me with her dazzling teeth and asked if I was leaving because of something that she did. Her question caught me unawares. I apologized, but still, I changed seats because I wanted to sit alone.

This guy who came to sit beside me was a little older, though it is quite difficult for me to tell people's age here in America. A simple rule of thumb that has worked for me is what I call *by their hats you shall know them*. Older gentlemen tend to wear hats no matter the weather.

He sat beside me and sighed the way the old tend to do as if the mere act of living and breathing exhausted them.

I noticed he was struggling with putting his box in the overhead compartment, so I took it from him and helped him put it up there. The box felt quite light.

"Thank you, I appreciate it," he said.

"Not a problem, at all," I said.

He extended his hand.

I shook his outstretched hand. He winced and muttered

easy and smiled.

"Such a strong grip you've got there. I am not a spring chicken anymore. My entire body is now fragile."

"I am so sorry," I said.

"There is no need to be sorry. I once had a grip like yours," he said.

I sensed that he was going to engage me in a lot of talking and I began to worry a little bit. The reason why I didn't mind sitting alone was because I liked the company of my thoughts when on the train.

"I can tell you are not from here," he said.

I groaned internally, but I smiled at him.

"How do you know that?" I asked.

"Your accent, to begin with," he said.

In this country you could walk into the train on your head and sit on your ears without a second glance from most people, but open your mouth and speak with an accent and get ready for comments, compliments, or sometimes being thought a fool.

I admitted that I was an alien, and that immediately put him at ease—or did I only imagine seeing his shoulders unclench.

"I knew it from the way you helped me with my stuff and the way you are dressed that you are not from here," he said.

I ran my eyes over myself and wondered what it was about my clothing that said the word *alien*.

"Forgive me for not introducing myself. My name is William. Remember it is William always, never Bill."

I told him mine.

"That is quite an unusual name," he said.

"It means that it is an honorable thing to work with iron," I said to him.

"Wow. That's amazing. I wonder why we can't have

names like that. Only the Indians, oh sorry, Native Americans have such names. They used to be called stuff like Big Wind, Dancing Bear, Crazy Horse, Wounded Knee, but nowadays even they have started taking our kind of names, like John Smith."

I didn't have the heart to tell him that my own name was not different from Smith's. We are both descended from people who work with iron. I could have told him about other names that denoted a profession too, like Baker, Wood, Milner, Chamberlain, and Cole, but I didn't.

He brought out a refillable water bottle and took a little sip like a bird. He looked at me, replaced the cap of the bottle, and put it on the tray in front of him.

"You'll discover that when you get to my age you have to be careful what you take in. No sooner do you take a sip than you have to rush to the bathroom to evacuate. Sometimes you get to the bathroom and you have to coax and persuade the damn thing to come out and oftentimes all you get for your effort are a few little drops."

I nodded and smiled. Too much information, I said to myself.

"But you know one thing about you guys that I like, you never age. No never, you just remain the same from year to year. You are lucky to have the kind of genes you have. Now if only we could have your kind of genes. Look at me, how old am I and I am already falling apart?"

Just then the conductor lumbered in. He was a big, burly, beefy-faced man who looked like an ogre in an illustrated children's book.

"Tickets, please. Tickets, *Ladiiieees* and *geeeentlemen*," he bellowed.

He checked the old man's ticket, perforated it, and handed it back to him.

I handed him mine. He looked at it, puffed out his cheeks, and said my name out aloud.

"I need to see your ID," he said to me.

I had not heard him ask anyone for an ID before me. He simply took their tickets, perforated it, handed it back, and thanked them.

Did I just imagine it or did the old man sitting beside me just wink at the conductor?

I handed him my ID. He looked at it suspiciously and skeptically. He turned it from side to side. He made as if to put it under his nose and sniff it. He then handed it back to me without any thank you.

I sighed. I started to feel a little hot and sweaty all of a sudden.

The old man was smiling at me. I did not smile back.

"One thing I like about you guys is that you obey the law. It must be an alien thing. See how you were very polite to that guy. You didn't argue. You did what you were told. I wish we could do more of that in this country, you know, follow the rules and do what we are told," he said.

What politeness was he talking about? The conductor had picked me out for special treatment simply because I had an alien sounding name. But, again, I did not want to argue with the old guy.

I brought out my wrapped lunch and was about to dig in and then I remembered my manners.

"Join me," I said.

It was customary in my culture to invite someone who met you while eating to join you. It was typically a theatrical performance in fake politeness. It was expected of you to make the invitation and the invited was expected to decline and say they were already full and then in turn you had to tell them to take just a little and they were expected to thank you and insist that they were not really hungry after which you went back to eating your meal in peace.

"You mean you are ready to share your lunch with me? Isn't that the most amazing thing?"

I extended it to him since I could see he didn't quite know how to act in this theatre of politeness.

He brought out his own lunch.

"I have my own lunch. See, this is what I keep saying, some people think aliens are bad, but I disagree. There are things we can learn from each other. See, how you were willing to share your lunch with me? That is something we could all learn to practice. We are taught to share in kindergarten, but no one actually shares in real life."

I watched him eat his lunch with no apparent pleasure. He was still eyeing my own lunch.

"You know what the problem is these days, right? We have to watch everything we eat. My parents didn't watch everything they ate, yet they lived longer," he said.

I bet if I told him that I grew my own potatoes in my backyard and made my own fries in my kitchen he would believe me and it would make him happy. I wondered if he knew that cultures that showed hospitality to strangers tended to be conquered and overrun by those same strangers with time.

We were both done with our lunch and the train was lurching forward, if ever so slowly. He turned to me and smiled and began speaking.

"You know one thing I like about you guys who come to this country from out there? You have such interesting lives. Your life stories, ah, they are something else. Look at my own life; there is nothing remarkable about it. I lived in the same Cape house like all the other kids I grew up with. We all went to the same elementary school and were taught by good old Miss Hassett. Same middle school, same high school. I was on the track team in high school and that was where I met my wife. We were both outcasts as it were. We were the unpopular kids, so we gravitated towards each other inevitably. I tried going to the community college for a day, but had to leave when on the first day of class the teacher told us to gather around in a circle just like I had done in the first grade and play a little game he called Icebreaker. I left and got hired as a trainee machinist in a factory less than two miles from where I was born. I worked in that factory all my life. I never missed work for one day. It was hard work, but it paid alright. See what I mean? What a boring life I have lived."

I did not see what he meant. Boring life? What boring life? The outline of his life that he just drew for me was interesting and spoke to everything that made his country different—stability and the fact that hard work pays a decent wage—but he didn't know this. Maybe he knew but took it for granted like the more fortunate tend to do.

Turning to me, he touched me.

"So there's this little Thai Food restaurant where I go to eat sometimes. I like eating foreign foods when the weather is cold. The way I see it if I can't travel to those warm places my tongue can take me there! So the little guy who owns the place likes to sit with me and talk. Every sentence he makes, he punctuates with *God bless America* or *America is a great country.*

"So I was talking to this guy, this owner of this Thai restaurant, and one day he began to tell me his life story. He was born in Laos. So technically he is not Thai. But he says it confuses people, so he sticks to Thai. So he was telling about his life. He said he was seventeen when the communists took over in his country and he was conscripted into the army. They took him to another part of the country, the northern part I think it was, to work in the building of a dam. He was not an engineer or anything so he was doing manual labor, felling trees and all that. But he didn't like the communists and was angry about the fact that he could not continue his education or earn good money to marry the girl he was in love with. So what did he do? One day he fled and went AWOL. He left the army and that part of the country and came back to the capital where he was born. He went into hiding and the only person aside from his parents who knew he had run away from the army was this girl he was in love with. One of the reasons why he had left the army was because he wanted to leave the country so he could earn enough money to marry her. So he was in his parents' house in hiding and this girl he was in love with came to visit him. He was so happy to see her. So he told her he had left the army and that he was planning to leave the country and that when he had made enough money he would come for her."

The train came to a jerky stop. Soon a high speed train zoomed past and our train waited for a while and started on its journey again.

"This girl, whom he was in love with, left his house that night and went and reported him to the authorities. She said she was a good communist and a good communist puts country first before father, mother, brother, sister, and lover.

"The next morning, soldiers kicked down the door of his father's house and arrested him. They sent him to an island prison for reeducation. In this prison you had to grow your own food and work in the farm for the government. He was in this prison farm but all he could think about was how he could escape. One day, he escaped. Now you think the story has ended right? Wrong. He escaped but he was caught. They caught him and trussed him up like an alligator and brought him back to the prison.

"He was tried and they were going to shoot him. They asked him why he was trying to escape. He said it was because he wanted to be with this girl who had betrayed him. He said that he was in love with her and that he could not think of her getting married to another man. They let him live because even the communists recognized the idea of love.

"Eventually, he finished his sentence and was released. He came back to the capital and the communist authorities made his father sign an undertaking that his son would be a good comrade, otherwise they would seize the father's house. His father signed. But this young man was restless and this time he bribed some people and he was smuggled out of the country. He was in a refugee camp in another country for some years and then a Catholic family with the last name Fish from Minnesota sponsored him and he came to this country.

"He trained as an auto mechanic but eventually realized that in this country we love to eat food from exotic places so he decided to open a Thai restaurant. He loves the ladies, this old guy. He is always happy and smiling and saying *God bless America* every chance he gets. He says the only thing he doesn't like about this country is that polygamy is against the law. I think in their culture in Laos they are allowed to marry more than one wife. He says that love is too good and big of a thing to share with only one person. See, what I mean? Look at how interesting his life story is? In his one life he's lived through war, prison, love, adventure, and escape. Compare it to mine. I am sure you have an even more interesting life story, right? No need to be shy. Accept it. Your life is more interesting than mine."

I was thinking about the story he just told me. What he romantically called adventure, the other man must have seen as human cruelty and suffering. I envied him the inimitable stability that his own life story represented. He could predict tomorrow and have a master plan that covered the next fifty years, whereas the man from Laos could barely plan for the next day.

I was thinking that I needed to use the bathroom but was also wondering if I should wait and do it before the train came to the final station. My co-passenger was obviously having the same thought, but had no plans to delay it. He stood up to go and so did I.

When I came back from the bathroom, the seat beside me was empty. The old guy was gone and so was his suitcase.

I looked around at the other seats wondering if he had switched seats while I was away, but he was no longer in that compartment of the train.

I decided to search for him by looking down the train but changed my mind. I realized why this place would continue to feel alien to me. Why had the old man left without saying goodbye?

The conductor was walking down the aisle of the train removing papers from the back of the seats and screaming something.

He was screaming Boston South Station is next . . . but all I heard over and over again was Neptune Space Station, Neptune Space Station, and then the train entered a tunnel and it all went dark.

Debriefing

Do not buy a car. Do not drive. Ignore advice to obtain an international driver's license before your arrival. American cops do not know what an international driving license is or for the most part they pretend not to know. What they don't know makes them angry. You do not want to face an angry American cop. Driving is a slippery slope. Driving is trouble. Driving is tickets. Driving is a cop asking you for your license and registration. Before you know it, you are standing before an elderly grim immigration judge.

❖

Avoid parties organized by our people. Arguments and fights break out over politics, over politicians, over girls, over anything, over nothing, drunken arguments. Especially after imbibing a cocktail of Hennessey and Irish Cream. Neighbors call the cops. Cops ask for identification. Remember you do not have one. I know we are a party-loving people, so if you think you can't live without it, go to YouTube, there's more entertainment on YouTube than you'll find at any Nigerian party. Nobody was ever arrested for watching YouTube videos.

❖

Avoid Rashonda and Shenika and her sisters. They once married, dated, or had kids for, and had their hearts broken by, our men in the past. They are on a revenge mission. They'll take out their hurt on you. They'll promise they'll marry you to help you get a green card. They will not. Ignore their avowed love for our local food. They'll tell you they love eating spicy food. They'll eat you dry, eat you out of the house and dump you. Besides they smoke weed. They'll expect you to pay for their habit. Weed is expensive in America unlike back home where you can get it for next to nothing.

❖

Avoid Chucks. Is that not a made-up name? Anyway, that is what he calls himself. His name is not the only dubious thing about him. He'll tell you he is in the auto insurance business. This is a ruse. Actually, this is what he does. He buys cars, insures them heavily, looks for a lonely road and drives them into a tree. After which he claims the insurance money and throws a big party. Remember what I told you earlier about Nigerian parties. He recruits new drivers at these parties. He will tell you that there is no risk involved. He'll assure you that all you have to do is wear your seatbelt and run into a tree. One of his drivers ran into a tree and broke a neck bone. He is still wearing a neck brace. Before Chucks became a car crasher, he drove around town in his beat-up Nissan looking for unsuspecting, inexperienced drivers who'll run into him so he can collect. Avoid him by all means. He has no honest bone in his body.

❖

If you must travel, travel by Amtrak. Trains are safe, buses are not. I mean safe from raids by the INS. Here's something that happened to someone I know. He boarded a Greyhound bus that was traveling from Chicago to Upstate New York. At the Greyhound bus station in Chicago there was this bunch of really boisterous kids. The boys were dressed in jeans and T-shirts, but the girls were dressed the traditional Somali way. Colorful scarves and cotton patterned wraps. It was a night trip. A few hours after the bus pulled out of the station, the bus was pulled over into a gas station by a detachment from the INS. They went from seat to seat asking people, *Where are you from? Do you have an ID? Identify yourself.* Soon they got to the row of the Somali kids. *Where are you from? From Chicago. I mean what country? America. Do you have an ID?* And the kids pulled out shiny U.S. passports. Avoid the bus, it is overcrowded, overheated, over-scrutinized, and accident prone. If you must travel, take the train.

❖

I suspect you will want to go to church because you are a man with problems and a man with problems needs church and prayers. If you must go to church avoid the American churches—they do not shout loud enough in the American churches. A person with problems needs a church where they can shout out loud enough for their voice to reach the heavens.

American churches do not announce jobs. The pastors do not know the places that hire those without papers. The pastors do not order people to go on seven days *dry* and or *white* fasting. They do not play loud music; they do not dance energetically and frenetically. I hear the African-American churches in the South do. But those are down south.

And while on the subject of churches—the church is not an opportunity to meet girls. The girls in the churches, the immigrant girls, are in the same rickety, leaky boat as you: they do not have papers, they are illegal, they are searching for someone to marry them for a green card. They'll not tell you this fact until you happen to mention it one day when you are both in bed and then they'll hiss like an angry snake and ask you *but why did you not tell me all this while, I have been wasting my time cooking for you?* And leave you on the

bed half-naked as they march out with righteous indigna-
tion, giving your door such a loud bang on their way out
and leaving the door wondering what it did wrong.

❖

People will urge you to go to school. They'll tell you
an American education is useful. That is so not true. It is
so 80s. You are here to hustle. If you must get any kind of
qualification, get a Nursing certification or qualification in
some medical field. A sick man does not care about your
accent. A helpless old lady needs strong arms, not a great
enunciation. There are many of those schools around. Get
into one and you'll qualify in eighteen months. I'll recommend the ones run by our people. They don't ask too many
questions and you can pay on the installment plan.

❖

If you need an immigration lawyer, never hire a Nigerian or Ghanaian lawyer. Get a white lawyer, preferably a
Jewish guy. He will ask you no questions so you will not
tell him any lies. Masquerades do not fear each other—I
need not say more. Besides by now you must have realized
that there are tribes in America. Remember when at the
port of entry you went to the black man in the booth and
you said he called you *brother*—a good white lawyer will
argue your case before his white brothers. Be prepared to
pay a bit more. Unlike the Ghanaian and Nigerian lawyers
they do not bifurcate their payments. The only payment
plan they adhere to is immediate payment. You must give
them a check before every meeting and before every court
appearance and before the signing of any document. I can
assure you they'll deliver. They get the job done.

❖

If you want to understand your new society better, you
should go out to a baseball game. Ignore invitations to play

five-a-side soccer with fellow immigrants in that obscure park on the outskirts of town. If you really hope to become a part of the society go to a nearby stadium and watch a baseball game on a Friday evening. Sing, "Take Me Out to the Ballgame" with the audience. Buy a beer and a hot dog, eat some cotton candy, try to catch the ball but do not try too hard especially if there is a kid around you trying to catch the same ball. Do not try to understand the game. It is neither cricket nor soccer. Just sit, relax, watch the people, sip your beer, and pay a little attention to the game. The good thing is that you are not obligated to stay until the end. Leave when you become bored or tired, but understand that you'll learn more about this society from sitting at that stadium with the smell of beer and nachos and screaming kids than you'll learn in any other place. Go on the Internet. Read up what can find on Barefoot Joe and Yogi Berra—learn some *Yogi-isms*. I have never met an American who hated baseball. As tea is to the Englishman, so is baseball to the American. I'll go as far as to recommend listening to baseball commentary on the radio. Play it aloud, let your neighbors hear what you are listening to; it will calm them and put them at ease about you.

❖

Avoid buying your groceries from the African store. Their stuff is overpriced anyway, and they'll rip you off. Train your palate to adjust to American food. There are affordable alternatives in the grocery store if you know what to look for. Eat lots of kale and spinach and collards. Winters are long. Your body will miss all the tropical vitamins but the vegetables will help compensate. Do your own cooking. Not only is it cheaper, it is healthier. As you'll soon find out, burgers and fries will not do you much good. Your cholesterol level will rise, your blood pressure will hit the roof from all that salt and fat, you'll sicken, and you are not likely to have any health insurance, so eat healthy. Still on the subject of your health, exercise moderately, stock up on Theraflu and Vicks VapoRub just in case you fall sick. The mosquitoes here do not carry malaria, so you do not have much to worry about.

❖

Dress well. Dress properly. Dress the way you wish to be addressed. Ignore that entire pant on the nape of the butt thing. Leave that to Little Wayne and all those guys on rap videos and the guys in prison. I am not saying you should spend all your money on clothes; all I am saying is that you should spend a little money on the right kind of clothes. *Dress preppy.* Not my words, but sage advice someone gave me many years back. Chinos pants and button down shirts. It is in your own interest to dress this way. It is reassuring. It makes you less suspicious. If you don't believe me, walk into your local Walgreens in sagging black jeans, black hoodie, and sneakers and watch the security guy follow you all over the store. Go back the next time dressed preppy and watch him smile and greet you with a *Hello, buddy.*

Since you'll not be driving, I suggest you invest in a good winter coat. Do not skimp on this. You can buy one on a layaway plan. London Fog is a good brand. You do not want to suffer from any cold-borne illness. They do to the black man what tropical illnesses do to the white man.

Talking about the bus, riding buses is a big hassle especially in winter. Their schedules are crazy. Looks like the auto companies want every American to drive a car. What makes the buses worse is the *bus people.* Your first thought would be that the buses are great. You'll think the buses are clean. You'll think the buses are not that bad. This is because you are still making the transition from the public buses back home. I remember them with their mobile pastors who pray for everyone in the bus and then pass little envelopes around for donations. With their medicine hawkers whose little pills cure TB and gonorrhea and chickenpox. Where if you are unlucky you could get your pocket picked either while rushing to board or struggling to alight.

American buses do not have those issues, but they have their own issues. Most municipal buses are filled with *crazies*. They may not bother to wash themselves or brush their teeth, but they feel compunction to lean into your face and start a conversation with you. *I am a user, you know. Not proud of it, but not for nothing, you know, it is what it is.* Buy an iPod. Blast your music. Do not engage in conversation. Do not smile.

❖

To join or not to join? Village associations, town associations, state associations, country associations, continent associations. They have them here. All sorts. They meet once a month or once every three months. Different names, same parole. You pay a membership fee. You pay a monthly contribution. Someone hosts the meetings. The host provides food and drinks. There is usually a Christmas party. In the event of a birth, you get a cash gift. In the event of the death of a parent, you get a cash gift. In the event of your own death, they are responsible for flying your body back home for burial. Quite frankly, I think you'll be better off with life insurance.

❖

Take accent reduction classes. Many people will tell you they don't know what this is—I do. I took one and that did help me a lot here. When I speak, people can hardly differentiate between me and a native-born speaker. Not

speaking the way Americans speak is like a dead man re-
fusing to speak in the language of the dead. Don't be deceived by all that false cooing by old ladies—*oh, that's a
lovely accent where are you from?* Some lady once told me
that when you speak with an accent people pay more attention to what you are saying. What she failed to add was
that they also speak to you very slowly having concluded
that you are an idiot.

❖

Buy a $1 lottery ticket every Friday. You are not likely
to win, but hey as they say here, *you never know* and *you
have to be in it to win it.* Avoid the casinos. They have some
of the saddest people in this country. Do not be deceived
by their inviting names. I know a guy who started going
to a casino out of loneliness. He couldn't wait to get out of
work and head up to play the slot machines and the black-
jack. He had not yet heard the expression *the house always
wins.* He would win a few dollars and put it back in. He was
soon taking payday loans to gamble. He promised himself
he was going to stop. One evening he drove straight home
from work. The first time in many months. He made dinner, poured himself a drink, watched a little television, and
went to bed. He said at first he thought he was dreaming.
He saw flashing lights, then the dings, tings, and pings. It
was like the lights and sound of the casino were right there
in his bedroom. He jumped out of bed, picked up his car
keys, and drove straight to the casino. He got money from
the ATM and began to play. He lost everything. He lit a cigarette—back then the casinos still permitted smoking—he
smoked the cigarette halfway and dropped it on the thick
rug. He drove home. The next morning he turned on the TV
hoping to see the news that the casino had burned down.
No such luck. Once again the house had won.

❖

I would have wished to guide you through this maze of a country by hand myself, but as you well know, I'll soon be gone. Voluntary deportation, that is what I took instead of prison. Voluntary indeed—an oxymoron. But as they say here, *it is what it is.*

Focus Group

#1

One thing that creeps me out about aliens is that they usually have large heads. Their heads typically look like they are too big for them, like a three-year-old lugging an oversized suitcase at the airport.

And they have this funny way of speaking, like they have a bee right up their tiny noses. I have never heard any of them speak with an indoor voice. Maybe they use a normal voice when they think no one is listening. But the ones I've seen, they always speak in this guttural, squeaky voice. The cool thing about when they speak, though, is that it comes off as *glubglubglubglub,* but then there is usually a subtitle and I guess there is some guy on TV who speaks their language because the subtitle would translate into something that makes sense like, "I Come in Peace." They usually speak in short precise declarative sentences. I never saw an alien tell a joke. Is it that they don't have a sense of humor? Like what happens when three little green men walk into a bar . . . ?

#2

There is this thing about their skin color. It is green. But you know a sad kind of green. Not the green of plants and forests and trees and leaves. A kind of weird green like the green of being sick. Sometimes the green glows in the dark, but not in this cool way, but in a kind of way that weirds you out, like a ghost-mode green glow, you know, not Sharpie green, not Day-Glo green, but old-lost-crayon-with-the-skin-peeled-off kind of green.

Why can't they just be white like everyone else? You know, how hard is that? I understand that their planet is hot. I think that's great; you can just have a tan all the year round, like Hawaii right? How hard is that? Look at all the problems in our world today because some are black and some are white—now if you add green to that equation you are bringing more problems into the world. And honestly, I think a cooler color for them would be gray. Gray like what you get when you mix white with black. That way everybody will see a bit of their own color in them and that would be so cool.

#3

They come across as so scientifically advanced. They always have these jets that travel at the speed of light, and the jets don't even use gas but are powered by converting whatever energy or force-field that surrounds them as they zip around at supersonic speed.

And one other thing, they are so good with gadgetry—like all the stuff that they have is usually capable of doing tons of stuff all at once. Their watches can tell the time, check the weather, and then the very next second turn into a dangerous weapon blasting dangerous rays and eviscerating everything in its path.

They must study a lot of Math and Physics and other stuff from kindergarten. I think that there is something we need to learn from them because they say among the countries of the world we are like number *what?* in Math and science, so why can't we just copy their model? We can start teaching our kids Math and Science from kindergarten and before you know it we'd be number one and your watch could begin multi-tasking in all kinds of cool ways, like tell the time and forecast the weather and tell you where to park and if as you are parking and a would-be carjacker comes to steal your car you could just zap them with a dangerous laser beam from your watch.

#4

I have not really given it much thought but the thing that I notice about them for the most part is that they don't have a sense of fashion. You know what I mean? They are not stylish. They look like they are always dressed in a costume for a middle school play about the Middle Ages. Don't they like have fashion designers? I get it. Not everyone can wear designer clothes, but we can all still try to look decent. What's with the shiny, gaudy clothes that always have high shoulders and wings like Icarus?

Look, if I am popping over to my next door neighbors' I always try to look decent. Now, these guys are coming to visit from their planet that is billions of miles away from ours, why can't they dress for the occasion?

#5

So obviously they have found a cure for cancer. I say this because I have never heard that any one of them died of cancer. Considering that they have such extreme temperatures in their planet one would have thought that they would suffer from cancer, but they don't, so that is really something. I think that they should be willing to share their knowledge with us. You don't think they get cancer? Fine. So how come they don't get cancer? What is it about them that makes them not get cancer? Is it what they eat? How much they sleep or don't? Is it something in what they drink? I think that this is the kind of information that they should be willing to share with mankind; otherwise anybody that tries to get this same information from them by force gets my vote. Who of us has not lost a dear one to cancer? It is the only reason why I think we should draw closer to them. Otherwise they mean nothing to me. They are only little green men after all, aren't they?

#6

Out of curiosity let me just ask you this first. Do they like have families same as us? I have never really seen like an alien family that includes father, mother, and kids. Sometimes they have wives, but their wives often walk unsmilingly behind them dressed in purple robes with pyramid-shaped headgear. They never converse with their husbands. I probably saw one of their babies once but that one came to stay with a family here on earth. So if they were such great parents, I don't think that their baby would run all the way from their own planet down to ours to live with some family down here.

So I think that is something they can definitely learn from us. Slice it however you want to. We are very family oriented. If you arrived from another planet today and landed your aircraft, hovercraft, spaceship, call it whatever you want—you would meet human families at the mall, at the beach, in restaurants, just about anywhere you go. So, in my view, they need to be like us. You know what the Russian writer said—all happy families are alike. We are all happy families and this is why we are all so alike.

#7

They don't have a democracy. That is one thing I know for sure. They come across as people who live under some kind of autocratic dictatorship. They are obviously used to a command structure with a single all-powerful ruler who calls all the shots. We don't operate that way. We believe in one man, one vote, no matter the size of your head. And it is a kind of leveler and has kept our union strong.

I think they need to come over here, see how our government works and then take our system back to their planet and shake things up over there. They would be happier for it. A democratic citizenry is a happy citizenry.

I think that is all I have to say. Let me add this. I fought in a couple of wars so that people all over the world could have liberty. All the countries where people had no liberty, their government soon collapsed and their citizens went into the streets burning flags and stuff until they became democratic. So there is a lesson for them right there. They should embrace democracy or one day on their own planet their citizens will set fire to whatever is the equivalent of flags over there and demonstrate on the streets until they have one person, one vote. That is all I have to say.

#8

You must give the human race credit for something. We have clearly been evolving. We always work towards getting better. Our ancestors invented fire by striking two stones together—since then we have come up with countless and uncountable ways to get fire. We keep evolving, we keep getting better, we keep improving and we don't believe we are even there yet. But tell me this; I have been seeing pictures about these alien guys. I have watched movies about these alien guys. I have read books about these alien guys. After all these years nothing seems to have changed about them. They look the same. They speak the same. They move the same way they have always moved—two steps at once, always in lockstep. Is it possible that the difference between you and us is that we keep changing while you remain the same?

Look at all our inventions. Our earliest computers were so huge they needed so many hands to move them. Nowadays you can fit some computers into your pocket. This is the way the human race rolls. I am not trying to be boastful here, just taking pride in our accomplishments as a species.

But as for you guys, your spaceships all look the same way they have always looked even when I was a kid. Your technology sounds the same with your equipment always beeping and flashing lights. It is quite possible that one is a little behind when it comes to news about your technological advancements; so, tell me, what are the new frontiers that you have conquered since? I'd be very curious to know how you have brought about new changes in mobility. Are your ships traveling at higher or lower altitudes? Are they traveling at faster speeds? Have you improved your propulsion force? These are genuine questions because, the way I see it, change is what has made us the superior beings that we are in the universe.

#9

Here is something that has always bothered me about your species. How come you folded your arms when we decided that one of your planets was no longer a planet? You accepted it just like that. I tried to imagine if someone somewhere came over here and told us that we were no longer a country or that we are not qualified to be a country. We would consider that the equivalent of somebody walking into your house and pissing in your living room. Will you condone that? How come you guys didn't see the signs when we first started belittling you by calling you the "dwarf planet." That should have been the signal. You needed to know that much sooner rather than later you would become the non-planet.

But let us go back to the beginning. We named you. Yes, we gave you your names. To name is the first claim of ownership. It is quite possible that you guys have a different name for yourselves, but we don't know that. So if you do, you could start by announcing it to us.

So if one day we wake up and we decide that we are taking over the planet that formerly used to be known as a planet but is no longer one we hope you will not be angry. We named it. We unnamed it. And now we own it. It is pretty straightforward. We own all kinds of territories and we will simply be adding to the variety of the territories we own.

#10

What do aliens eat? What does their diet consist of? Do they eat three times a day the way we do? Are they vegetarian? Are they herbivores? Do they eat meat? What type of meat do they eat? Are they cannibals? Do they juice? Do they eat healthy? Are they always feasting?

You may wonder why I raise these questions. I ask because there is so much we can learn about other species from their diet. From their diet, for instance, we can begin to understand why they live forever and we can then infer that by doing the same—following their diet, that is—we can begin to live forever as species, thereby ensuring that we are not wiped off the face of the earth.

If you watch them closely you'll notice that they never look overweight. They all look trim and fit. What could we learn from this? They must follow a strict diet regimen. Species that control what they eat control everything else. So we can see that that the possibilities are endless for humankind. Their diet may help us fight the obesity epidemic so we can all shape up and not ship out of our beloved planet earth.

There are so many other things connected to their eating habits that could be of benefit to us. How do they grow their foods? Do they practice sustainable agriculture? Do they practice crop rotation? They come from a dry planet; so how do they irrigate their crops? Water is one of the scarcest commodities today. All the trouble in the drier parts of the world is caused by the fight for scarce water resources. So there is so much that we can learn from them. Imagine what we can accomplish if we can seed the clouds with rain and make it rain at the press of a button. We will be able to grow enough food to feed all of mankind. If man can feed himself believe me most wars would be over. Forget all the talk about wars being fought for ideology—the main reason why we have all these wars is because people are scrounging for scarce resources.

It is also quite possible that they do not eat at all. In my view this is even better news. If they don't eat, then how is it that they do not feel hungry? What we are looking at right here is an end to world hunger. If we can end hunger, we have solved the biggest problem in the world. People fight wars every day over food. All the political upheaval in the world can be traced to food, one way or another. So, what we need to ask is why they do not get hungry. Is it that they pop a pill three times a day or even once a year?

#11
To me the thing is that I think we really want aliens to exist, but have we thought of the fact that they actually may not exist? It is quite possible that we would wish that they

existed, but in actual fact those other planets are just like totally barren with no form of life out there. I am trying to be logical here—think of the number of years that the earth has been existing and then imagine that aliens have been trying to get in touch with us all these years without any success. It is not possible.

Another possibility is that they exist in a dimension that is invisible to the human eye and human inventions, so it is quite possible that we don't see them but they see us and are laughing at all our efforts to search them out. So what I think is that we may just be looking at the Sphinx from behind. And remember if you look at it from behind, the Sphinx would just look like a collection of stones.

If they can see us and we can't see them, this raises the possibility that they may not want us to see them because they know all about us and our ways. It is like you want to go out on a date with someone and a few days before the date you are allowed to look at this person through some kind of monitor. So you see them but they don't see you, right? You can see all the stuff they do when they think that no one is watching them. It is very likely that what you see may gross you out so much that you want to have nothing to do with them any longer. That is the way I see it. It is just possible that we think we are the ones pulling the strings but all the while they are the ones peering at us and shaking their heads and saying we do not want anything to do with these folks.

#12

I think aliens were once like us. Do you know what I mean? They were once people, but then they evolved to a higher level and so they are more conscious beings. Having evolved in their mental sphere they have gone on to make advances in almost every area. Think of their advances in Engineering, Astronomy, Chemistry, and Physics. They have left us behind simply because they were once like us. It is the same way we have evolved beyond the Neanderthal man, and he now looks to us like we were not once like him. It is the same thing with aliens. I believe that we will one day advance to where they are today, but who knows by then to what extent they too would have advanced? We should not feel bad about it. If you doubt my theory, let me just give you one little example: You know we have made some advancements in aeronautics so we now have airplanes and jets that fly faster. But they were the first ones to do that. Their flying saucers and what we naively called UFOs were already moving at the speed of light before we launched the Concorde jet. So the way I see it, it is only a matter of time and mankind will become aliens.

Child's Play

I can't remember the exact age when my sister and I began to do it. We would go behind our large family compound to the clearing behind the house. We would look around to make sure no one was watching. All the grown-ups must have left for the farm and the market. We would hold each other's hand and begin to spin on our feet. Faster and faster we would spin until all the trees and houses around us turned into an unrecognizable blur and then the ground would open up and we would find ourselves in a new place where we would play with our new friends all day.

And then the hours would go by super-fast and we would find ourselves spinning again and we would be back home in the space behind the compound. We would be so tired from playing with our friends all day that we immediately fell asleep after dinner and snored heavily until morning.

I remember one day blurting out to my mother the fact that we usually went to play with our friends in another world when she left for the market. I don't know why I said it. She looked at me; her eyes immediately widened and grew teary.

"Ah, this child has malaria," she said. She touched my forehead with the back of her palms and shook her head.

"Your head does not feel hot, but you certainly have malaria fever. Maybe it is hiding. Let's go give you a cold shower."

She fetched cold water in an iron bucket and after giving me a cold bath told me to go take a nap.

I never mentioned our trips again.

Playing in the other world was a whole lot of fun and made the kind of play my sister and I used to play at home look childish.

Before we started going to the new world to play, my sister would sit in the sand and I would sit in front of her and she would gesture to me to get the pots and pans we needed to start cooking before everyone got home from the farm.

I would gather a few empty cans of discarded Peak Milk and De Rica Tomatoes and bring them to her.

She would indicate that today we would be cooking rice and stew and so we needed to get two cooking fires going. She would get the cooking fires ready by putting two or three pebbles together and putting some tiny sticks in between them. She would pour water into the sand and pour the wet sand into the pot then we would begin to add stuff to the food on the fire. If she was feeling adventurous she would pluck some basil leaves from the garden and add them to the pot. When the food was ready, we picked up short sticks and pretended they were spoons and began to eat. We would sometimes build a house by pouring water in the sand and molding the sand into shape to form walls.

This type of play was actually no great fun, as we would discover when we began to go into the other world to play. They did not play pretend. It was all real. But still fun.

The greatest thing about playing in the new world was that we could play as loudly and as crazily as we wished. There was never any adult asking us to tone it down or come back into the house because it was time for lunch. Besides, it never grew dark.

Our new friends never spoke a word to us, they only gestured, but we understood them perfectly. That was great for my sister who had never uttered a word since she was born.

When we indicated that we were interested in shooting, they handed us real guns. We looked up at the sky and they understood that we wanted to shoot at a flying thing. They clicked a button and mechanical crows filled the sky with their dark wings and threw shadows over us. Aiming our guns up high we began to shoot and no sooner did the mechanical birds fall to the ground than they'd shrug almost as if nothing happened and their wings would come together and they would fly back into the sky only for us to shoot at them again. My sister, who would normally cry at the sight of blood when we killed a chicken for Sunday lunch, enjoyed shooting the birds immensely, surprisingly.

If we wanted to build walls, our playmates provided mortar and cement and concrete mixers and trowels—they even gave us plumbs to see that the wall was straight. We would build and then, when we got tired, we would climb on the bulldozers that were standing by and begin to demolish the walls until there was no sign that the walls were once standing.

There were days we did not feel like going back to earth. We could tell that our friends would not mind our staying to play with them forever. On such days we would only just manage to return home a few minutes before our mother got back home from the market.

She would look at our tired faces and hiss.

"A child that comes back home with oily lips from eating outside will one day come back home with bloody lips," she said to us on such days.

"Go do the dishes. I have to get dinner ready. Someone has to work even if all you people know is to play."

We never felt hungry in this other world. We never felt thirsty. When we played near the house it was not unusual to run into the house for a drink of water and to quickly grab a snack—sometimes an orange, some chin-chin, ground-nuts, or a quarter loaf of bread in a transparent plastic bag.

Our playmates did not run home to have a drink either. We never wondered about this. We did not wonder about many things.

Where were their parents?

Where did all the bulldozers and guns and bullets that we played with come from?

Why did they live in mud-adobe houses and why did the houses glow bluish even in the daytime?

Why were there no animals running around their houses? No chickens, no goats, no ships, no dogs?

We became tired of shooting mechanical birds that never died and of walls that were eventually flattened. On this day we came to play and gestured that we wanted to make a fat man out of cement. Our playmates gestured that they would prefer that we made a thin man and then feed the thin man until he became a fat man. This sounded like more fun and we nodded in agreement.

We molded the thin man's head and legs and his body, but we did not forget to make his mouth big because we were going to feed him until he grew fat.

Soon the thin man whom we were going to feed until he became a fat man was ready.

But where was the food? What were we going to feed him? We thought lots of carbohydrates like *fufu* and yams and bread would do the trick.

Our new world-playmates had a different idea.

They mixed cement in a concrete mixer and began to pour the cement into the mouth of the thin man. As he drank the cement he began to grow big. But all his body was not growing big. Only his stomach was enlarging. We watched as the thin man became the big-bellied man and our eyes grew with wonder and we almost forgot that we should go home and that our mother would be calling our names. We hurried to leave. We went to our spinning spot.

We began to spin and soon we surfaced near our backyard.

Mother was back and she was fuming. We still had specks of cement dust on us from the other world.

"Where have you children been?" she asked. "Look at how dirty—you look like children without mothers. Run inside this minute and go take a bath. I keep warning you children that the dog that refuses to heed the hunter's whistle will soon be lost in the forest. Only a stubborn fly follows a corpse into the grave," she said, and spat.

We ran into the bathroom and washed up. On the floor of the bathroom the cement from our skin formed a gray concrete mini-pyramid and we pushed it with our big toes until it dissolved.

We decided that we were not going to the other world to play for a while. Our mother's proverb about the stubborn fly was still fresh in our ears.

We struggled not to go, but we could imagine our playmates in the other world building a pillar that would be higher than what the eye could see. We wanted to be there.

We decided that we would spin but we would not go to the other world. We would spin and just at the point at which we would be in the other world we would stop spinning. Is it possible for the whirlwind to change its mind in mid-spin and no longer be a whirlwind and dissipate into ordinary dust?

We could not stop ourselves and soon we surfaced in the other world. We could tell from their manner that our playmates had missed us. There was no time to waste. They had a new project in mind. There were no trees here and they wanted us to make tree sculptures with branches. Using our fingers we drew a tree with branches on the red earth for them. They looked at our drawings in wonder and then got to work. First we gathered the pieces of steel together. They brought out welding instruments and we started with the trunks and then the branches. This was fun but a lot of work.

They used the bulldozers to dig holes in the ground where the giant trunks would be planted.

It looked to us like this project was going to be a different one. Each thing we had made in the past we eventually demolished at the end of the day. This particular project looked quite elaborate and we went about it with the mindset of people creating something permanent.

We soon had all the tree trunks lined up in a row.

But trees were not trees if they had no branches and leaves.

It was getting late and we had to leave.

We spun and spun.

Our playmates watched us. They would usually wave excitedly when we were leaving, but was there a certain kind of reluctance in their waving today?

For some reason our spinning took longer than usual, but eventually the ground opened up and we found ourselves back home.

Our mother was like an angry frizzle chicken on that day.

"Today, you children will know who is mother and who is child in this house. You will tell me today whether I was the one who lay down and made you or if you both wandered in from the evil forest into my womb. I did not kill my own mother and if you children think you are going to kill me with worry, you will be the ones to go first."

"We are sorry," I said.

"Do not be sorry now. It is not yet time for you to be sorry. You are the ringleader. Since your sister can not speak for herself, you must drag her everywhere you go with you."

"We will not do it again," I said.

"You will do it again, but you will not have the chance to do it again. From today going forward everywhere I go you must go with me."

"To the stream . . ."

"We will go with you," I said.

"To the farm . . ."

"We will go with you."

"To the market . . ."

"We will go with you."

"To the river . . ."

"We will go with you."

She was beginning to calm down.

"There are people in this village with seven children; their children have not driven them out of this town with their troubles. I have only two. Even your sister has refused to open her mouth and speak. What have I done? Who have I offended? What did I do wrong? I go out to find what you children will eat. What is it that keeps the mother hen clucking in both rain and sunshine if not the search for what her children will eat?"

We felt sad and felt truly sorry for our actions.

From that day we would go with mother wherever she wanted to go. We were glad to go with her, but she was not happy to have us trailing behind her. We made her a little less nimble on her feet. It was only a matter of time before she got tired of dragging us along with her and told us to stay home and not wander off and play too far away from the house.

It was only a matter of time that we grew bored. We were soon missing our friends. We derived no pleasure from our old cooking game.

Then one day I said, "Maybe we don't know how to spin any more. Let's spin a little and see what happens."

We began to spin. Things soon began to blur. We were one with the whirlwind. Soon the ground opened and we found ourselves in the other world.

We could see that our playmates were not happy. The trunks of the trees were still lying the way we left them.

As soon as they noticed that we were ready, they became excited. We began to make the branches for the trees. There were so many tree trunks. We needed a lot of branches. It was as if the more branches we made the more the branches that were needed.

It was time for us to go.

We stood up and went to our spinning spot. We began to spin. Our feet felt like molted iron. We would not spin. We were stuck in one spot.

Our playmates beckoned for us to return.

There were more branches to make.

And after the branches?

We would have to make the leaves. Thousands and thousands of leaves to cover many trees.

We went back to our playmates.

Was that our mother's voice we were hearing above ground, wailing, weeping, and crying?

"Where are these children?"

"Where have these children gone?"

"It is growing dark and they have not come back home."

"It is growing dark. So dark," she cries.

"Over here it never grows dark," our friends said. "It is always daylight."

The tree trunks were calling out to us, "Where are our leaves? Make us leaves. What are trees without leaves? Give us leaves. Hasten, give us leaves."

Who Is in the Garden?

His wife came into the house like a mini-hurricane, sweeping the curtains to one side with her left hand and not even pausing to drop her purse before attacking him.

"Why did you turn on the generator? Eh, why are you running the generator by this time of the day?"

She did not wait for him to answer. His mouth was still half-open mulling his response.

"Don't you know that the cost of fuel has gone up? Don't you know that we need the generator to power the air conditioner through the night so I can sleep and wake up to go to work and earn money to buy petrol for the generator?"

"I only turned it on to watch the match. My team Liverpool is playing. It is only for ninety minutes," the man said.

The wife snorted. She tossed her purse on the worn-out sofa. She hunched her shoulders. For a moment she looked like a boxer gathering herself to let fly a punch in the ring.

"Your team? Did I hear you say your team? How many times have they called you to share money from their winnings with them? Your team, indeed."

The man sensed a minuscule opening and tried to think of a response that'd lighten her mood and lessen the thick tension gathering in the room. His wife sensed this too. Pausing was a mistake. She decided to intensify her onslaught.

"How does your watching these grown men kick a ball around help put food on our table? At least the players are making more than enough money to feed their own families."

"Let me go and turn off the generator," the man said.

He had no real plans to turn off the generator. A player from the opposing team had just been given a red card. Liverpool would be playing against ten men. This could put Liverpool in front even if only with a lone goal.

But his wife called his bluff.

"Turn it off. At least if there's any fuel left it should carry us for a few hours," she said.

He reluctantly went and turned off the generator. His day was ruined, or whatever was left of it. The game would have given him enough energy to survive his wife's onslaught from the dinner table to the bedroom. Now, deprived of the high from the game that would have carried him through the remainder of the day, he felt deeply bereft.

He contemplated going to read last week's issue of the newspaper, the Tuesday edition that carried job vacancies, but he suddenly had no strength to see those jobs. These were jobs that he was qualified for but was tired of applying for because he knew that the positions were already filled and that the adverts were mere formality.

What he found even more painful were the chirpy, smiling faces on the "Moving Up" column. Some of the smiling faces were former colleagues and people he knew from past professional association. He knew he dared not step out until it got dark because of the stares from the neighbors who even though they knew he had no job would still ask him if he was back from work already.

He could have gone to one of the Viewing Centers, but they charged a cover fee and the crowd was oftentimes a rough one. There was no way of knowing who was supporting who until you opened your mouth to cheer your team and the man sitting beside you got angry and tore into you.

He decided to look at the garden. It was actually his

backyard, but he was the one who called it a garden. He had had grand plans for it. He had thought he could plant some fruit trees in it and on one side a small orchard for growing his favorite dwarf pineapples but all that ambition had dried up like the arid soil in the garden.

He pulled the curtains aside and looked into the garden. That was when he saw it. It was right there in his back garden. It was sitting *majestically,* to borrow his wife's grandiloquent phrase. He could not believe his eyes at first. What was that in his garden? How long had it been there?

At the moment that people's lives change, most people are usually able to recall with total clarity what they were doing. Sometimes they feel a certain heaviness in the moment preceding the incident. In his own case he felt some certain lightness. He felt the weight around his shoulders lift, suddenly, like a hand had grabbed them and tossed them far from him.

❖

His mother-in-law was the first person to knock on their door the next morning. She entered the house singing a Christian hymn. The man did not find the words of the hymn familiar though the tune was somewhat recognizable. It was not impossible that she had composed the hymn on her way to the house. She was the type of woman who believed that the difference between man and beast was man's ability to improvise.

"Look at what the Big Man in heaven has done. Look and see what he has done. I told them, didn't I? Years ago when you came to knock on our door to tell us that you saw a beautiful daughter in our garden that you wanted to pluck—meaning you wanted to marry my beautiful daughter—there was nothing my ears did not hear. My ears heard so much they hurt. He is too short. A woman can be short, but a short man? How can his wife respect him when she can see the top of his head when she's talking to him? What about that giant beard on his face? Men with huge beards, you cannot trust them. They are always up to something; they have all sorts of evil plans while they tug at their facial hair. Nothing wrong with a full moustache but a full bearded man, now that is something else."

The man watched his mother in-law sing and dance and talk.

"Ah, people from his ethnicity never marry only one wife. It is even worse when the wife is not from their part of the world. They must marry a second wife or even a third. Do not say I did not warn you," a neighbor had said to her.

As the man watched his mother-in-law sing and dance in his sitting room, he wondered if it was the same woman who had recently sworn not to set foot in his house again until he worked hard and took care of her like other good sons-in-law. In a way though, she was right. She was setting foot in his house now because things had changed.

The thing in the garden had changed all that, he realized.

His wife offered her mother tea and bread, but she looked at the food and hissed.

"What am I eating for; can't you see that my stomach is filled with joy? I don't need any food. All we need to do now is to pray. Ah, this is the time to pray. We must thank heavens for this great good fortune of yours. We must also pray against the evil eyes of enemies looking at you with envy now that things are going to change or rather now that things have already changed for you. We must pray for the eyes of your enemies to go blind. And my daughter, you need to pray even more because men change when their fortunes change. Let us all kneel down and begin to pray," she commanded.

His wife called her job to let them know she was going to be absent. She was so solicitous towards him that morning. She asked him what he wanted for breakfast. She did not yell at him as she used to when he added an extra cube of sugar to his Lipton tea. Back in the day she would have screamed at him and berated him for having a sweet tooth when he could not afford to give her a sweet life.

He whispered to himself to enjoy this, her newfound largeness of heart.

She was all of a sudden full of suggestions.

"You will need a haircut, my love," she said. "You know you must look the part. People are going to start visiting soon. We will begin to know important people. Appearance does matter."

He nodded his head in agreement. He knew that in the past, when he would insist on having a haircut on the last Saturday of every month, she used to mock him and ask him who was looking at his hair to know whether it was cut or bushy.

She talked about the things that must be done. Changing the old brown rug to a new wine-colored one. She said brown was a dead color. She also said that he needed to change the furniture.

He was reluctant to ask, but he finally did ask where the money was going to come from. He knew the thing in the garden meant a change in their fortunes, but it didn't translate into hard cash, at least not yet.

When he asked the question, he nearly caught a glimpse of her old yelling and quarrelsome affect, but she caught herself just in time and began to lecture him in the tones of an inspirational text.

"Money has become our servant; it is no longer our master. We can now call it and say do this and it will do it. Soon people will be begging to loan us money because of this thing that fortune has bestowed on us. Those who have more get more, and we have joined the group of those who have more," she said.

She said that after he had rested they would talk about protecting the thing in the garden. He told her that he did not need to rest, but she insisted. She told him that it was important that he rest his head now that they still had the time to do it. It was when he went into the bedroom and she came to join him that he understood what she meant by *rest*. Not in their entire married life up to that point had she shown such enthusiasm in bed. In their past life when he summoned the courage to bring up sex, she would ask him if that was all he thought about even with the difficult times they were passing through.

The next night the money people came in their suits and shiny quiet cars. They knew that money was a subject best discussed under the cloak of darkness. They began to speak to the man and his wife in the language of money.

The language of money was a new, if not strange language to them, but they loved the way it sounded and they loved the musical sound it made in their ears.

"What you have here in your garden is extraordinary, and we think that the first thing we should do for you is to package a little loan to tide you over while you plan on how best to monetize it," they said.

They used words that in his past life always came with charts.

Monetize.
Amortize.
Collateralize.
Instruments.
Float.

Even the words that he had some familiarity with had new meanings in the mouths of the money people.

He only nodded gently while his wife nodded so vigorously that he was afraid that her head was going to fall off.

At the end of the conversation they brought him a thick sheaf of papers to sign.

He remembered that at his last job it was the fact that he had signed a big sheaf of papers without reading the small print that had put him in trouble. He had spent five days in a police cell and months going in and out of lawyers' offices and courts until all that was left of him was this little house with a garden that he had built with his savings.

That weekend they threw a party, the kind of party the weekend tabloids referred to as a Talk-of-the-Town party. There was food, lots of it. There were all kinds of drinks. There was music and there was dancing.

No invitation cards were sent out. It was that kind of party. Everyone was welcome because there was enough to eat and drink, and then some.

Those who did not know of the good fortune that had come to them by way of the garden talked about them in tones filled with wonder.

"They have arrived. And look at how fast they arrived. One minute they had nothing to eat and the next minute they are feeding the entire street. Isn't that something? That is truly something I tell you," one said.

People came to pay obeisance to them like subjects in a drama before a king and his queen. Their voices were filled with admiration and their tones dripped with awe even as they picked meat off their teeth with toothpicks.

The man and his wife sat in elevated decorated chairs smiling and waving at their guests—not saying much, as was the habit of the rich. As silence was the currency of the rich, loquaciousness was one thing that was freely available to the poor, and they spent it without looking back.

Now it was the turn of a smallish man who lived down the road. You could tell that he was a man on his second bottle from the way his words rushed into and after each other.

"It is not because I have eaten your food and I am drinking your wine. Ask anybody, I always said it each time you walked down our street with a newspaper folded neatly under your arm. I always pointed at you and told people—that is a man with a plan. Trust me, I know someone with a plan when I see them and I could tell you had a plan, though the exact nature of the plan I didn't know. But see what has happened now—I have been proven right."

The speaker paused as if waiting to be contradicted by someone, but all were smiling and nodding their heads in agreement including the celebrant and his wife. The speaker walked away in self-congratulation.

Another came forward and stretched out his two hands towards the celebrants.

"I congratulate you and I congratulate myself" was all he said, and went back to his food.

The woman who came after him went straight to the man's wife.

"Do not forget me, my friend, now that heaven has smiled down on you. Remember that I was always there for you when it was rough," the woman said.

The man's wife was a little confused. She could not remember seeing that face before in her life. But she continued to smile as more people came forward, greeting and thanking them.

"Well done."

"Thank you for deciding not to eat alone."

"May the heavens who did this for you also do the same for us."

"One with God is with majority."

"We know today, but no one knows tomorrow."

"This life is not hard. It's us humans that make it appear like it is hard. Look at you people now. Look at how you have decided not to hide the good that has come into your lives, but to share it with your fellow humans. Why would it not be well with you? Who says you could not have decided not to share with anyone and kept it all to yourselves?"

Many were the salutations and congratulatory messages that began this way:

"To be honest with you . . ."

"Heaven knows that . . ."

"Truth to tell . . ."

"I cannot lie to you . . ."

"Between you and me and heaven . . ."

Again, the man was touched by all the outpouring of good wishes and kind words. He had no idea that people thought so well of him. But he also wondered if it was not the new him that they loved. The old him barely received a nod of acknowledgment from some of the folks that were coming to bow before him today.

When he whispered this to his wife, she frowned at first then quickly recollected herself.

"This is who we are now. We must not overthink things. We must learn to enjoy it all," she said.

It was well past midnight before their last guest left. The wife wanted to go to bed, but the man held her hand and led her to the thing in the garden. It glowed phosphorescently, throwing a halo around the man and his wife. They both held hands and went down on their knees like worshipers before a religious icon. They bowed their heads together, and yet again they bowed before it and continued to bow even as dawn approached. The thing in the garden glowed down on them even as their own faces glowed with pride.

On the Lost Tribes of the Black World

Since Professor Dekalb published his much talked about and celebrated paper on the lost tribe of Koma in *Black Anthropology Review* there has been a sudden spike in interest concerning some of our beloved continent's less known civilizations.

What many do not know is that there are quite a few past African civilizations of which scholars have little or no knowledge. They do not know who they were and how they lived. Much of the information about them is lost to antiquity and the mists of time. This is therefore an attempt to bring to the notice of the world—or to exhume if you will—one of these lost civilizations.

The Konga

All that is left of this tribe of great warriors, musicians, and dancers is the Konga drum—misspelled Conga by quite a few scholars—which is rightly named after them. They were unique in the use of drums to communicate with each other. Husbands had their drums, wives had female drums, and children had their own baby drums. It was these drums that every person used to communicate with each other. The Konga never once opened their mouths to speak, but rather let their drums speak for them. For this reason they were known as *the tribe who used their drums as their tongue.*

They were as dexterous at using their drums for communication as they were for using these same instruments to entertain during feasts, burial ceremonies, naming ceremonies, and so many other festivities.

The beauty of the Konga culture was that women and men considered themselves equal and this was because at birth each person was given their own set of drums to beat. Neither of the sexes was better at pounding the drum than the other since they both started learning to beat and caress the instrument at the same time.

There were hardly misunderstandings among the Konga because drum sentences were precise and tended to make their points easily without wandering or digressions. It was difficult and complicated to tell lies with drums—the hands tended to tremble, the sound that emerged became feeble and it was almost as if the drum itself was reluctant to cooperate with the owner. The Konga were honest people, they were fearless and courageous and perhaps one should add that they each marched to the sound of their own drum. Ideas of truth, honesty, and right conduct were drummed into the ears of the young at a tender age. A Konga saying has it that the feet do not resist the tune of a drumbeat that they heard in infancy.

Did the Konga have quarrels among themselves? Hardly, if any, because it was often difficult to keep pounding out in anger, the palms began to hurt, the arms grew weary, and soon each party began to beat a reconciliation beat and then the feet had no choice than to obey with dance steps.

Some people have questioned the Konga habit of sleeping with their drums—cuddling the drums while asleep the way babies in modern times cuddle their teddy bears for comfort. For the Konga people, though, the drum on the bed served more the same function as the telephone by the bedside, within easy reach to send and receive messages. Do not forget that their drums served as their mouths, and while it is expedient to keep the mouth shut while asleep, it was also necessary to have it with you just in case you wanted to scream at an intruder.

And the Konga habit of burying their dead upright while holding their drums? They believed and rightly so that one should march boldly into the next world while announcing themselves with their drum. This may be the reason why they never placed their drums lying face down, but always had it standing erect at all times.

We owe all that we do today regarding the humane treatment of animals to the Konga tribe. Because the Konga used all kinds of animal skin in the making of drums—no animal was considered too lowly, from the bat to the elephant—they made sure that they killed the animal while doing as little damage as possible to the skin. They also believed that the skin of an animal that died unhappily would lead to a drum that sounded mournful no matter how vigorously you played it.

It is not possible to talk about the Konga people without talking about the phenomenon of the Silent Drum That Must Never Be Beaten. This giant drum which stood in a grotto surrounded and shaded by coconut trees was revered and venerated. People knew about its existence and where it was housed, but nobody dared to go and touch it. The name of this drum was known to be invoked on different occasions. If someone wanted to vow about their honesty among the Konga, it was not uncommon to refer to the Silent Drum That Must Never Be Beaten as their silent witness.

When in danger the Konga people have been known to cry out to the Big Drum That Must Never Be Beaten to come to their rescue. An ancient prophet and seer of the

Konga people once prophesied that the day the Silent Drum would sound would mark the end of the Konga people. She also said that as long as the Silent Drum remained silent the Konga would continue to flourish like the frangipani.

To modern ears that are used to hearing nonstop talk and speech and the ever constant flow of word-lava, it is rather difficult to imagine how the Konga managed to say all that they had to say using only their drums. The truth with the Konga was that they hardly ever wasted words. Note that there is a vast difference between a refusal to waste words, which suggests precision, and a paucity of vocabulary. The Konga for instance had over fifty different words for *drum,* but it was rare for anyone to use more than the basic word for it.

There are a lot of reasons why we should study the Konga and their civilization. What they did for the humble drum is much more than what the Inuits did for snow. They took a lowly instrument like the drum and made it their mouthpiece. They provided the DNA for the text message. All the things that the text message thinks it invented, like the use of abbreviations, were of course first used by the Konga.

The Konga taught us to treat all people as equal and with dignity. The man who could speak had no advantage over the person who couldn't. Have drum, will communicate, was their mantra.

You only need to look around you and listen hard and you'll hear the beat of the drum of the Konga people resonating and sounding off in our language. There are traces of it though you might miss them if you don't listen carefully.

We drum things into people's ears to make them remember.

We drum up support for all the things and people that we support.

We bang and beat the drum for our ideas.

We drum up excitement for all the little things that excite us.

We sometimes beat like a drum when we become tired, old-fashioned, and boring.

We occasionally hit the back of the drum, jumping around with old information that we think is new.

We applaud achievements with a resounding drum roll.

It is the Konga who gave us these expressions that resound through our language.

There were no thieves among the Konga. Yes, you heard that correctly. The Konga never stole from each other. It all started with the fact that if you stole someone's drum, of what use was it going to be to you when you were not able to beat the drum? Would you hide it under your bed? Would you hide it in your room? Would you secretly beat it when you thought the entire community had gone to sleep?

When it was realized that it was pretty pointless stealing a drum, the idea became applicable to every other thing. There was no need to steal. Simply ask to borrow the item from your neighbor and you will get it.

Backbiting?

None.

Gossiping?

None.

Conspiracies?

None.

There was really no way to do all of these things in secret as long as the drum was the instrument of communication.

But one day a new generation began to grow up and, as new generations do all over the world, they began to ask questions.

We have legs and we use them to walk.

We have ears and we use them to hear.

We have two hands and we enjoy using them to beat our beautiful drums.

We have our nose and it helps us to breathe and keeps us alive.

We have our mouths, but we do not use our mouths to do anything. Our tongues are stuck to the roof of our mouths.

Our tongues dormant and unused. Why can we not put them to use?

They asked these questions and many more. They were impatient for answers, as the young are wont to be.

The older people tried to calm them down, but they wanted answers and they wanted them now.

Mouths mean talking and talking means trouble, the Elders said to them. Talk means gossiping and backbiting and rumors and lying and bearing false witness. Look at how peaceful our lives have been all these years. We don't have any trouble among ourselves because we keep our lips sealed and let our drums do all the talking.

But the young people would not be appeased. They wanted to talk with their mouths. Soon even the sound of the drums became cacophonous. Each side tried to make itself heard.

Finally, the Elders got tired and gave in to the young people's demands. That was how the Konga slowly began to lose their innocence. Though they had control over the drums they did not quite know how to control their tongues.

The Silent Drum That Must Not Be Beaten watched over them and was very sad.

It is not possible in a short paper such as this to go into details about the decline and fall of the Konga. Let us leave that for a symposium discussion in the future.

Love Affair

Finda was leaving Providence. She was moving back to Delaware to live with her father. Her grandmother had suffered a stroke. Her grandmother was in a bad shape and could barely control the saliva that dribbled down the corner of her mouth to her chin. Her grandmother cried every day. She would say, "Look at me, Finda. My God in heaven, why do you leave me to become like dis. My God, why you lef me for pipu to laugh at me? Take ma life, le'me come and be with you an' res'."

Finda loved her grandmother and even in her present condition she did all she could to make her comfortable. She cleaned her with a warm towel and sat by her, helping her to clean the spittle with a clean white wash cloth.

This was despite the fact that grandmother had told her that when it was time for God to destroy the earth, as he promised that he would in the Bible, the first people he was going to destroy were the le'bians.

"You Finda ma chil', you come to America and you see all the *fine fine* things and profession in America. You don't say you want to be a nurse or doctor or school teacher. The only thing you say you want to be is this thing they call le'bian in this America. You are lucky, if we were back in our Lofa County back home in Liberia, they would have given you to a chief or king to be his junior wife, who knows maybe wife number eight."

"Grandma, I don't like men," she would tell her grandma when she was in the mood to argue.

"You think me I *like* men?" her grandmother asked her.

"Nobody *like* men. All men do is take, take, take. They take your beauty, they take your body, they take your money and when they take everything from you and they have nothing else to take they take another woman as they wife or girlfriend."

"So if you don't like men why did you marry, grandma?"

"You this chil' you make me laugh. So if don't like something, does that mean you don't do it? Look at me, I don't like the cold in this Providence. Rhode Island too cold for me, but what do I do? I stay here and manage myself. I wear many clothes for winter and look like masquerade and people laugh at me but I don't mind them. I even tell them, if you have more coat to give me, I'll take it and add it to mine."

"Yo, grandma."

"Don't tell me *yo*. You keep going *yo yo yo* like the African American kids. All the time I tell you not African American, you African from Lofa county in Liberia. We all come here because of the war, if not for Charles Taylor, Prince Yormie Johnson and all the strong men who fight the war in Liberia you will be in Liberia and maybe by now you would have more than two children that I can carry."

"OK, grandma, but you mean there are no people like me in Liberia?"

"What you mean people *like* you? You are jus' confused. If you were back in Liberia and you tell your family you le'bian, you know what they gonna do? All your uncle gonna gather together and tie you up and invite some strong and powerful young men to lie with you after which they pack all your stuff and give you to a king or chief to marry.

By the time you get to your husband house you forget all the foolishness and you think of your children. You think there are not many women who don't like men in Liberia? But you know what the women do? They work so hard and they become rich like the men. They build they own house and they have many stalls in the Waterside Market so the men come to respect them and the men cannot be able to kick them around like football."

"Wow, grandma, that's cool."

"Grandma don't care if it cool or hot. All grandma want is for you to finish school become LPN nurse or CNA nurse and work hard and take care of your grandma before I return to my Maker. Look at me, how many years you think I got here on earth? This Rhode Island cold is not good for me. At least I know when I get to heaven there is no cold there."

Now her grandma was so sick she could barely talk. She was barely able to hold down her oatmeal at breakfast and looked at the television without much comprehension. Her grandma who used to be a huge fan of the *Maury Show* and would call her to come and see the people disgracing themselves on the show.

"Tell me, Finda, these people on *Maury Show,* how much are they paying them to be on the show? I'm sure they getting thousands of dollars. You think dem have family? If dem have family why dem family let them come on *Maury* and disgrace dem family name like this on the *Maury Show?*"

"It's a free country, grandma," she would say to her grandma.

"Don't tell me it is a free country. Nothing free here in America. You pay for everything. You pay for light. You pay for gas, you pay sewage bill, you pay the pipu that pick up the trash, you pay for water, even now senior citizen pay on the RIPTA bus, but everybody say free country, free country and yet nothing free."

"Grandma, you too funny."

"I'm not funny. I jus' saying the truth."

But she was leaving Providence and she had to see Shay. Her father was coming with a U-Haul to take her back to Delaware with her grandmother. Her dad's wife would take care of her grandmother until she got better.

She knew she needed money to see Shay. She would need to buy a dub sack of good weed from D'licious and not the shitty half dime shwag ditchweed they usually smoked. She knew that once she told Shay that the weed was from D'licious, Shay would come running. She just wanted them to have that last smoke together and take sips from that small bottle of Henny and talk about the future. When she got to Delaware, after her high school equivalency exam she would train to become a CNA. Her grandma was right. She would work hard and get a job and buy a car and have her own house and she could be with Shay and they'd be a couple. Shay needed some convincing sometimes, but she would convince her.

"I ain't no lesbian anything. I'm just a freak and I like you, though you ugly," Shay would say to her.

Shay would often say stuff like this to her and laugh. Shay would touch her face when she said this and take a drag of the weed and hold the smoke down and hold it down some more until her sclera began to glow a dull red, slowly shifting from their preternatural whiteness.

"If I'm ugly why you with me *tho*?" she'd ask Shay.

"Because I love you and you treat me nice and you ready to go to bat for me at the doff of a hat."

"But you ain't no lesbian?"

"No. I'm your girl. I ain't ever gonna be nobody else's bitch but yours. I don't go with no other women except you."

"Whatevs, kid, as long as you are with me and not hanging out with your so-called cousin."

"Jamil is really my cousin. I swear to *Gad*."

"If he's your cousin, how come you go on dates?"

"Dates?"

"Smoking weed together, ain't that a date?"

"You too funny, G," Shay said.

Finda knew she had to earn some good money to make that final party with Shay happen. They had both met at the Upward program, a kind of fake school that you could attend to get a high school equivalency diploma. The state of Rhode Island gave them vouchers to buy stuff if they attended classes for a month without any absences. They provided free books and backpacks and winter clothes and beanies and even Baby Phat fur collar coats.

"Ah, only in America they pay you people to go to school and yet some people will not go. In Liberia, school children pay school fees. God will *really* bless America," her grandma would exclaim.

She needed to earn some money. Shay deserved to be given that last good treat. She was going to give her something to remember so that when she was not here to keep an eye on her she would remember that she had her *mans* and her *mans* always treated her right.

She texted Kim Dior.

Kim Dior was that kid at the alternative high school program that wore genuine Timbs and carried a real Michael Kors bag, not the knock offs they sold on Manton Ave. She wore some expensive Chanel perfume that lasted all day and trailed her everywhere she went. Half an hour after she'd been in the bathroom, the aroma of her perfume still lingered; anyone who walked in after her would know that Kim Dior had been there. They were friends, sort of, and she smoked so they bonded at that level. Most people at the program said she went with men for money, but they never called her a *thot* like they called the other girls who went with the boys at the alternative high school.

Once she had gone to smoke with Kim Dior. It was some good shit and it left her feeling really mellow. Kim Dior had turned to her and asked her if she wanted to earn some money.

"Hey, Kimmy you know that's not how I roll," she had said.

"Yo ain't even gonna hear me out?

"OK, tell me what's up?"

"So there's this older Guat guy that really likes me. He's a sweet older guy. He has a landscaping business and all. He lives in Central Falls. Sometimes he gets a hotel room and he invites me over."

"I don't go with guys, Kim Dior."

"I know that, but see this old Guat guy is way too old to do anything. I just take of my clothes and he looks at my body and then I put my dress back on and he gives me a couple of hundreds."

"Wow."

"Yeah, he's a sweet guy. He doesn't speak much English, he's from Guatemala."

"That's kinda cool, but I don't do no shit with men," Finda said.

"Nobody is asking you to do shit. You just come with me, take off our clothes, and chill with this sweet Guat guy for a bit, then we put our clothes back on and pick up our benjamins and we *dip*."

Finda knew men. She knew how they loved to talk all sweet and then before you knew it—bang, you down and they kicking you.

She remembered the boys back in Wilmington. They had invited her to the party. She had been excited. She was in middle school and these were high school kids. They were kids she knew from way back and their families knew each other. She had been shocked when she got to the party and she had been the only one except for the boys.

"Yo, you know what's up. We can do this the easy way or we can do it the hard way. Take off your dress and we can all party and have fun or we can make you do it. That's what's up," one of them said to her.

She didn't want anything to do with no men. They start all sweet and stuff, but it never ended sweet. Men tasted like vinegar or more like the castor oil her grandmother gave her to drink whenever she had cramps or said her belly hurt.

But she wanted to have that last party with Shay, which was why she had texted Kim Dior and asked if her proposal was still open.

Kim Dior had texted right back and said her offer was still open.

Let's do it, she had texted Kim Dior.

Her idea of a hotel was a place that was fancy and had clean linen and uniformed people who worked there, but the hotel they went to meet the old Guat guy looked like a strip mall and had no name to boast of.

Kim Dior came in an Uber and she had jumped in hoping they'd be in and out within half an hour, but when they got to the hotel they had to wait for the guy. Kim Dior was obviously used to this and played Candy Crush on her phone while she smoked.

"He be here soon. I told you he runs his own business. You gonna like him. He is cute."

"I don't really care about him that much, Kim Dior.

Let's just do this quickly. I need the dough."

"Yeah, me too. But don't act like you don't care. He don't like girls acting weird around him. He can be a little paranoid, too, so you have to act really chill around him. Sometimes he does this thing where he looks into your purse and asks if you're are a cop."

"He smokes?"

"I wish. No, he don't smoke weed," Kim Dior said.

The Guat man soon arrived in a truck. A Ford F150 black truck that was shiny and glistened as if it had only been bought yesterday.

They went into the room. A tiny room with a bed and a super tiny bathroom. There was no TV in the room. What kind of hotel does not have a freaking TV, Finda wondered?

"You brought a fren' huh?" the Guat man said and smiled, taking off his hat and rubbing his bald pate.

"Yeah, I know what you like," Kim Dior said.

"Is she eighteen, your fren'?"

"Yeah, she's a big girl, wait till you see her titties, then you know if she's eighteen or not," Kim Dior said and laughed.

The Guat man laughed and seemed to relax.

They both began to take off their clothes.

"Take it off slow," the Guat man said.

They began to take their clothes off slowly and methodically.

His eyes swept over their bodies—up and down, up and down, over and over and side to side.

The Guat man nodded at Kim Dior. Kim Dior went and sat on his legs and he whispered something to her.

"Hey, G, he wants some *extra*," she said to Finda.

"Some extra what?"

"You just lay with him on the bed so he can *finish*. He's gonna tip well."

"I don't do that shit. I don't care if he *finish* or not."

"Your fren' got temper," the Guat man said.

"Kim Dior, you said we only need to take off our clothes. You didn't tell me nothing about *finishing.*"

"Don't worry, honey, I take care of you real good," Kim Dior said, and joined the Guat man in bed.

Finda picked up her clothes and went to dress in the tiny bathroom. She was tempted to shower but glimpsed the filthy towel and changed her mind.

When she came out of the bathroom, the Guat man and Kim Dior were fully dressed.

The Guat man brought out a husky wallet and peeled off four fifties.

"No tip?" Kim Dior asked.

"Your fren' not nice to me," the Guat man said.

"You too cute," Kim Dior said and pulled the Guat man's bulbous nose.

The Guat man opened his husky wallet again and peeled out two twenties. Kim Dior snatched them up.

"Give one to your fren'. I'm really nice guy. I don' bite," he said.

Kim Dior blew him four air kisses, two for each cheek, and went into the bathroom. She sloshed Listerine around her mouth, spat it out, applied fresh makeup to her face, and they left.

In the Uber, Kim Dior told her that she was feeling this way because it was her first time.

"Is he not cute? He's so nice," she said of the Guat man.

Finda only nodded. The only two things on her mind were Shay and the money.

"I have some extremely cool clients, wait until you meet them, you gonna like them. We'll be rich together," she said.

She didn't feel like arguing. She didn't want to tell Kim

Dior that this was her last day in Providence. She did not see any need to do that. Kim Dior was not really her friend *like that*.

Kim Dior gave her two fifties and a twenty and smiled.

"See how much you made in less than an hour of work? Stick with me we gonna be rich, girlfriend."

Finda's mind was elsewhere.

She needed to call Shay and tell her that she'd be swinging by with some good shit from D'licious. She need to pick up a mini-bottle of Henny from the sip store down her street. Then she'd shower and dress up in her black jeans and her Chance hoodie and tie her do-rag and she'd roll. She'd spend many hours with Shay and they'd talk and make plans and roll and smoke and sip, then she'd head back to join her dad in the U-Haul back to Delaware. They were going to drive through the night and the next day they'd be back in Delaware. She didn't want to worry about what life was going to be like for her after that.

She messaged Shay on Facebook and told her she was headed her way with some good shit.

Shay was not reading her messages. Shay had this trick she did on Facebook Messenger where her read messages appeared as unread.

She began texting her telling her she was heading to the South side and would see her soon.

She did not want to see Shay's mom. The woman did not like her. She said Shay was a good girl and had made just one mistake. She said Finda was a negative influence on her daughter. Finda laughed at this. What a fine example she was to her daughter after three marriages. The only reason why she had a job was so she could keep her current boyfriend and herself in Newport smokes and E&J and have money to go to Twin River casino every weekend.

Even though Finda called her Mrs Jackson like she was some respectable person, she barely acknowledged Finda.

When D'licious handed her the bag of weed she opened the bag and smelled it and inhaled deeply and then gave him three tens.

"Ain't no need to do that, y' know what I'm sayin', this is good shit. Y'all know I'm legit," D'licious said.

"Just checkin'" Finda said and handed him the money. She watched him zoom off in his tomato-red Audi.

She decided to walk to the South side so that she could call Shay and tell her to get ready.

She called Shay over half a dozen times, but Shay's phone was obviously switched off.

Shay's Tracfone was always ringing and the battery drained fast. She sent her another message but there was no response. She decided to walk faster and then broke into a trot.

When she rang the doorbell it was Mrs Jackson that opened the door.

Mrs Jackson looked her up and down and told her Shay was out.

"Shay not here," Mrs Jackson said.

"Where she at, Mrs Jackson?"

"She a grown woman now, she doesn't need to tell me where she goin'."

"Please, Mrs Jackson, I really need to see her tonight," she said.

"Someone dead or someone dying soon?" Mrs Jackson asked—a wry smile appearing on her face.

"It is just that . . ." Finda said and trailed off.

"Jus' what?" Mrs Jackson asked.

"Oh, never mind, Mrs Jackson."

"Well, if you are not gonna tell me, I don't see how I

can help ya'll," Mrs Jackson said.

"I am moving back to Delaware," Finda said.

"Ah see," Mrs Jackson said.

"My grandma is sick and my dad taking us back to Delaware," Finda said.

"Your daddy?" Mrs Jackson asked.

"Yes, my daddy is here already. He's getting a U-Haul and we leaving tonight, Mrs Jackson."

"Ah see. Well the thing is Shay went out with Jamil. They goin' out if you know what I mean. But see when Shay comes back I'm gon' tell her you called and I'll be sure to give her your message," Mrs Jackson said.

"Thank you, Mrs Jackson," Finda said and turned and began to walk back home.

She decided to bypass Olney and go through the back streets in the cut. She soon got to a small bridge. It was the bridge over the Woonasquatucket River. She looked behind her. There was no one following her. She brought the small Hennessey bottle out of the pocket of her black Chance hoodie and hurled the bottle over the bridge into the creek. She waited for the sound of the bottle hitting the water or hitting a rock, but it didn't come. She cocked her right ear waiting for the sound of the drop, but it never came.

She switched off her phone and began walking back home.

The Home Companion

Congratulations. You have become a Home Companion owner. As you may already have guessed, we are one big, happy family. We know you have questions and we will answer them as efficiently and as quickly as you ask them.

You see, the Home Companion is not a product, neither is it a gadget. As you know, products and gadgets do exactly what they sound like. They are things around the house that serve a purpose. The Home Companion on the other hand is a companion—no gadget could ever be that. A quick example: Let's say you are a lonely bachelor with a sucky job and an even suckier life and your name is John. Now we are just being hypothetical here because we know you live a full life and have a fulfilling job. But just for our hypothetical purposes, John's grandmother bought him a Home Companion. John installed the Home Companion the previous night, but he's completely forgotten all about it until he walks in and a cheerful chirpy voice intrudes into his consciousness.

"You're back early. How was work today?" asks the Home Companion.

"Horrible day at work. My boss Mr Murgatroyd chewed me out again."

"Murg-a-troyd, what a sad name. I bet anyone who's had to carry a name like that around with them all their lives must be unhappy and would always look for ways to make other people sad. Murg-a-troyd."

John finds himself chuckling and his mood lifting after that little intervention from the Home Companion. "See, the Murgatroyds of this world always find willing receptacles in which to deposit their inner pains. You must never let yourself be a receptacle for him. Always be cheerful around him. Greet him with joy and ask after his family—you and I know he has none—but you bet he'd find it pleasing to his ego. Start calling him The Bossman in a non-patronizing way. Watch what happens. Watch him lap it up. Watch him eat out of your hands."

So John walks to the fridge to get himself his usual dinner fare of frozen pizza and a humongous bottle of Dollar Store root beer. Did he just imagine he heard the Home Companion make a discreet throat-clearing sound?

"If we want people to treat us better and show us some respect, then we must treat our body better. Why don't you and I prepare a meal? The process of putting a meal together feeds the soul, the body, and the spirit."

John shyly admits that he hardly knows how to cook.

"We could start with something really easy, like a shrimp and veggie stir-fry. Cooking is fun. Creative people get their best ideas while cooking. Let me walk you through it."

John dashes to the frozen aisle in his neighborhood grocery store and comes back with all the stuff for the stir-fry. The Home Companion walks him through the process in a fun way and he is surprised by the result.

"See, we did it!"

John enjoys a home-cooked meal for the first time and actually feels full and fulfilled. After the meal, he wants to turn on the television to watch *Wheel of Fortune*—he secretly crushes on Vanna White, wink, wink—and grabs a can of beer on his way to the remote. Another gentle clearing of the throat follows, almost imperceptible.

"Actually, do you mind reading to me tonight? I have no preference, but perhaps you could read me something that'd make my heart race a little, or my blood pound, or even make my skin tingle a little bit, or make me too scared to close my eyes—of course we both know I never close my eyes." This again, from the Home Companion.

John goes rummaging in the bin in the basement where he dumped all the books he bought from time to time at the Dollar Store. He would usually scan a few pages and lose the motivation to go on. They had titles like:

Towards a Better You.
Positivity and the New You.
Secret Keys to a Better You.
The Secret Is in Your Hands.
Open the Door to the Hidden You.

They all held promises to finding out the *you* that you didn't know was hidden somewhere within you and waiting to jump out.

He finally did find a title. A little novel that he had read somewhere was really good but had been overlooked by the entire world until it was recently rediscovered and had the breadth of life poured into it by some small paperback publisher and had suddenly grown wings and taken off.

John sat and read aloud to the Home Companion. He could not stop reading because the more he read the more he realized the overlooked novel was actually about him. It was telling his life story. The protagonist was him and he could not stop.

"We must get enough rest. Let us continue tomorrow," the Home Companion suggests ever so gently.

John went to bed for the first in as many nights as he could recall without having had a beer.

This was also the first time he did not get up at night

to go to the bathroom at least three times.

Although the Home Companion did not come with John to work, he could hear the voice in his head all day as it guided him. He even made a little joke to his boss, Mr. Murgatroyd. He was patted on the back by his boss. At the suggestion of the Home Companion he listened to Public Radio on his way to work and for the first time felt like not only did he know everything that was wrong with the world, he also felt like he could fix the world's myriad problems.

He couldn't wait to get back home and share gossip and news with the Home Companion.

❖

John couldn't believe how much his life had changed. He, the same John who had gone on what would be recorded as the shittiest of shitty Tinder dates. He recalled that he and the potential date had agreed to meet at Olive Garden. It was crowded when he got there. At the suggestion of a hostess, he sat at the bar.

He ordered a colorful drink while he waited for his date. All around him people tried to get to the bottom of bottomless salad bowls and seen the end of endless breadsticks.

At some point he had noticed the barmaid gesturing, but he had not thought much of it. The barmaid had asked him if he needed a refill of his colorful drink. He had responded in the affirmative while he looked at his quiet, unblinking phone.

He must have ordered his third colorful drink when the barmaid, obviously overcome by pity and consideration for his blood sugar, asked him if he was expecting someone.

He said yes.

She then told him that she didn't think his party was coming.

His *party*? How did she know they were a no show?

His party had been at the door earlier and had left, the barmaid said.

What had his party seen from behind that had made her rush away? Not even Mount Rushmore looked impressive from behind. When viewed from behind, the Sphinx was only a pile of stones, everyone knew that. It was why we had a face. No one looks great from behind.

These days he didn't bother with any dates or dating apps. He read Romantic poetry to the Home Companion. The Home Companion once remarked to him that Romantic poetry was safer than the search for real-life romance and one was less likely to have their poor heart broken by poetry.

He had also evolved into a wine drinker. Just a glass with his home-cooked dinner. He could tell the difference between Zinfandel and Zappruda, all thanks to the Home Companion.

His taste in music changed. He no longer listened to bands so obscure they could not be Shazamed. He now loved classical music and could tell the secret note in Beethoven's Choral Ninth Symphony that was lacking in the Eighth.

Would he change anything about his life now? Definitely not. What would his life had been like without the Silent Listener? The question only reminded him of that old joke that said, "Thank God for electricity or we'd all be watching television by candlelight."

The only question John often asked the Home Companion over and again was why had we not met each other sooner? Why? Why on earth?

All Our Earthly Possessions

Everyone had a cavernous bag filled with hope; we were hopeful that we would cross the water, the barriers, and border guards, that we would make it to that place where the lights shined. We harbored no doubt that when we got to the other side we would find jobs. We would work and earn money, some of which we would send home. We were hopeful that one day soon we would return home in triumph. We carried our few belongings in a tiny backpack, dark from passing through fire, hailstone, and brimstone, and more.

One of us had the picture of his brother, who lived where the lights shone. They were not actually brothers but distant cousins. They were not even cousins, they were from the same village and that was good enough. In the picture, his brother was everything that he hoped to be: big, brawny, strong, smiling, well dressed. He stood beside a car fringed by a huge pile of snow. The snow did not appear to bother this brother of his. He looked happy standing beside the car. Was the car his? Who knows? However, the way he stood beside the car seemed to establish its ownership. He wore a blue baseball cap that had two letters that looked like raised arms.

We all had prayers in our hearts, but it was not enough. We also had prayer beads and rosaries. Some of us wore our rosaries to sleep. While we slept, the rosary glowed in the dark, casting what we hoped was a halo of protection around us. Some of us had our prayer beads wrapped around our wrists when we were not counting them with our fingers.

We rarely missed the call to prayer.

One of us had an old copy of *Complete Football* magazine with him. Though he must have read that magazine cover to cover over a hundred times, each time he had a quiet moment he would peer into the magazine, perhaps hoping to discover some undiscovered hidden message.

We all had exercise books filled with telephone numbers—numbers of those we left at home—fathers, mothers, brothers, sisters, aunts, cousins, friends, those who worried about us and were anxious to know if we had reached our destinations, those who could not wait for us to get to our destinations so we could begin sending money home through Western Union and his younger brother *Money-Gram*. A few of us were lucky to have the telephone numbers of the people that we knew over there. I had my Bro's number, but it was not written on a piece of paper; I had memorized it. Even if you woke me up at midnight, I could recite his number with my eyes closed.

We all had images in our minds of what we assumed the other side looked like—clean streets, beautiful people, smiling faces, shops and supermarkets crammed and jammed with food and goodies. We harbored images of houses that were taller than palm trees, and images of trains that ran faster than bullets. We saw ourselves walking in these spotless streets, dressed to keep the cold out, strolling and laughing, carrying shopping bags and stepping with a spring and a swagger like we owned the streets.

In another part of our minds, we also had images of our return home. We flew back. Yes, we no longer needed to travel via this route of pain. We would be welcomed just as our cars pulled up to houses that had been freshly painted in preparation for our arrival. There would be music, food, electricity, and joy in the air. We returned, dressed, as we had pictured ourselves those many years ago. We had both arms raised, acknowledging cheers as we entered our houses to the sound of, *Welcome, welcome, great traveler, home at last, home at last.*

We still had thoughts about the girls that we loved and thoughts of the girls who loved us. We remembered the girls who had scorned us, and wondered if they would still scorn us on our return. We wondered if by the time we returned, we would still consider them as beautiful. We did not let this bother us for long because, in the mental picture preserved in our minds, they neither changed nor grew old.

We all had our phones. Phones with single SIM cards. Phones with double SIM cards. Phones with which we could browse. Phones with Opera Mini browsers. It was important that we remained connected, that we remained in touch.

We all brought along stories, stories of how our journeys began, of the things that our eyes had seen but our mouths could never say. We had stories about those we had met on the way. Some of whom we left on the way. We had stories that we shared to sustain ourselves, stories that we kept for later, so that we could tell others. We had long stories, short stories, stories we made up, stories we did not make up, stories we could no longer recall whether we made them up or not, because these stories had lived with us and had followed us on this long journey.

Though it was difficult, we still had the ability to make each other laugh. We gave each other nicknames. We mimicked the ways the other spoke. We made fun of each other's clothes and remembered that even in the heat and dryness of the desert, laughter could stretch out its cool hands and somehow soothe our brows.

We had memories. Memories from childhood. Memories from *before* and *after*. This was how we told our memories apart going forward. Through our lives, all that had happened and would happen would be separated by this experience under the giant signpost chiseled with the words *before* and *after*.

We still had our memories of things that happened in the sky. Like when an airplane flew past, and left a curly pillar of white smoke behind it, we had looked up and imagined the lives of the people sitting inside it. People eating and drinking up there in the sky. What manner of pleasure could be higher? Who were they? What did they do to be placed higher than those of us at the bottom? Would our feet ever get a chance to leave the earth's red soil and be suspended between sky and earth?

We despised the lack that had dogged our lives. We knew the unwritten words of the song called "Never Enough."

Never enough clothes. Sleeves too short to cover our hands even when it was cold.

Never enough cream in the jar. Using the middle finger to coax the little left in tight corners. Even when that was gone, pouring a little water into the empty jar and making do.

We had memories of drinking *Coca Cola* on special days, sharing the prized bottle with one friend, no, two friends, and sometimes even three.

We also had memories of the things that money could not buy: the smell of the red earth after the rain; the sweet song the rain bird sang when the weather was so dry that rubbing two blades of grass together could spark a fire; the aroma from cooking pots in the evening; the water from the rock, so pure, so clean, it washed off thirst and made you think you would never be thirsty again. We had memories of sitting by the fireside and eating roasted corn, of sleeping while it rained, dreaming of rain while we slept, and waking up to the sound of rain on the tin roof.

Memories so sweet.

Memories in Technicolor.

Memories so alive, so close, we could touch them if we stretched out our hands.

We had our memories of journeys. In our memories, journeys were the exclusive preserve of grown-ups. Usually, mothers went on journeys. Fathers went as well, but rarely and only for something very important. We remembered journeys as things to look forward to, not because we traveled but because our hopes traveled with the grown-ups when they left. Why the journeys of our mothers? Because they always returned with something nice.

We had hope. We knew fully well that to travel was to hope; hope that at journey's end was a rainbow, not a coiled serpent. We had hope in humankind.

We also had an unstoppable eagerness: an eagerness to see new people, smell new things and eat new food. An eagerness for our tongues to learn to curl seamlessly around languages that were foreign to us.

We had the wisdom and stubbornness of the he-goat who was reported to have said that traveling is indeed a wonderful thing; how else would he have found out that his father wasn't the only goat who had a beard?

We had a ringing in our heads, the wisdom from our long-departed ancestors about travels, traveling and the traveler. Their words of wisdom such as, *The traveler cannot afford to make enemies. The traveler who asks questions will never miss his way. Travel gives one the wisdom of the gray-head*. Finally, the one, we were taught in school: *Traveling is part of education.*

There were also the things that we did not have. We had no fears about the present, no fears about the future.

As far as we could tell the future held only prospects of all that was good, bright, and beautiful.

Some things we left behind. Some things we tossed out. Some things we put off for later to avoid distraction. Some things we swallowed, with plans to bring them up later.

We carried, in plain sight on our foreheads, dreams so bright and dazzling that you could see them from miles away.

Our nightmares were a different matter altogether. We had a lot of these. As we slept, tossed, and turned at night, screams emerged from our different throats. Colorful nightmares, we all had them.

We drowned in our nightmares. When we opened our mouths to scream we gulped down bucketfuls of water, yes, water. There were other times that we drowned in sand and saw ourselves choking on mouthfuls of sand.

At daybreak, the harsh sun emerged to clear our nightmares, and we suddenly became ourselves again. We refused to be fragile from the nightmares. We steeled our faces.

"How was your night?" we asked each other.

"My night was great. I slept well. I slept soundly. It was the brightness of the sun that woke me up."

We never mentioned our nightmares.

Occasionally, one of us said, "You know, I had a dream last night."

We drew closer. Was he going to man up and talk about the nightmares in the day?

"What was your dream about?" we asked.

"It was beautiful. In the dream we had crossed over to the other side and we were all well settled. We looked fresh and healthy and were glowing."

"Who else was in the dream?"

"You and you and you and you . . ."

And every single one of us raised our hands to ask if we were among those who glowed in the dream.

We wanted to be in that beautiful dream badly. We completely forgot that no one screams in beautiful dreams. Perhaps, we did not forget. Perhaps, we preferred the sweet lie to the bitter truth.

Then, the few things we did not have, we harbored no anger or regrets over.

None.

ACKNOWLEDGMENTS

Thank you to the editors of the publications in which the following stories first appeared:

Guernica Magazine: "Alien Enactors" and "Debriefing";
Los Angeles Review of Books Quarterly Journal: "How to Raise an Alien Baby";
Taste Magazine Summer Fiction Issue: "Feast" (published as "Alien Feast");
The Threepenny Review: "Mark" (published as "Alien Mark");
Zyzzyva: "Visitors" (published as "Alien Visitors").

My gratitude to Peter Conners and the entire BOA team. Thanks to Sandy Knight for the amazing cover design. My gratitude to the writer Chris Kennedy in Syracuse. Thank you to Maik Nwosu in Denver. My gratitude to Bill Pierce in Boston. Thank you, Victor Ehikhamenor in Lagos. Thank you, Meakin Armstrong.

About the Author

E.C. Osondu is a winner of the Caine Prize, the Pushcart Prize, and other prizes for his short stories. He is the author of the collection of stories *Voice of America* (HarperCollins, 2010) and the novel *This House Is Not for Sale* (HarperCollins, 2015). His writing has been translated into Japanese, Icelandic, Belarusian, German, Italian, and others. Born in Nigeria, he lives in Rhode Island and teaches at Providence College.

BOA Editions, Ltd.
American Reader Series

No. 1 *Christmas at the Four Corners of the Earth*
Prose by Blaise Cendrars
Translated by Bertrand Mathieu

No. 2 *Pig Notes & Dumb Music: Prose on Poetry*
By William Heyen

No. 3 *After-Images: Autobiographical Sketches*
By W. D. Snodgrass

No. 4 *Walking Light: Memoirs and Essays on Poetry*
By Stephen Dunn

No. 5 *To Sound Like Yourself: Essays on Poetry*
By W. D. Snodgrass

No. 6 *You Alone Are Real to Me: Remembering Rainer Maria Rilke*
By Lou Andreas-Salomé

No. 7 *Breaking the Alabaster Jar: Conversations with Li-Young Lee*
Edited by Earl G. Ingersoll

No. 8 *I Carry A Hammer In My Pocket For Occasions Such As These*
By Anthony Tognazzini

No. 9 *Unlucky Lucky Days*
By Daniel Grandbois

No. 10 *Glass Grapes and Other Stories*
By Martha Ronk

No. 11 *Meat Eaters & Plant Eaters*
By Jessica Treat

No. 12 *On the Winding Stair*
By Joanna Howard

No. 13 *Cradle Book*
By Craig Morgan Teicher

No. 14 *In the Time of the Girls*
By Anne Germanacos

No. 15 *This New and Poisonous Air*
By Adam McOmber

No. 16 *To Assume a Pleasing Shape*
By Joseph Salvatore

No. 17 *The Innocent Party*
By Aimee Parkison

No. 18 *Passwords Primeval: 20 American Poets in Their Own Words*
Interviews by Tony Leuzzi

No. 19 *The Era of Not Quite*
By Douglas Watson

No. 20 *The Winged Seed: A Remembrance*
By Li-Young Lee

No. 21 *Jewelry Box: A Collection of Histories*
By Aurelie Sheehan

No. 22 *The Tao of Humiliation*
By Lee Upton

No. 23 *Bridge*
        By Robert Thomas

No. 24 *Reptile House*
        By Robin McLean

No. 25 *The Education of a Poker
        Player*
        James McManus

No. 26 *Remarkable*
        By Dinah Cox

No. 27 *Gravity Changes*
        By Zach Powers

No. 28 *My House Gathers Desires*
        By Adam McOmber

No. 29 *An Orchard in the Street*
        By Reginald Gibbons

No. 30 *The Science of Lost Futures*
        By Ryan Habermeyer

No. 31 *Permanent Exhibit*
        By Matthew Vollmer

No. 32 *The Rapture Index:
        A Suburban Bestiary*
        By Molly Reid

No. 33 *Joytime Killbox*
        By Brian Wood

No. 34 *The OK End of Funny Town*
        By Mark Polanzak

No. 35 *The Complete Writings of
        Art Smith, The Bird Boy
        of Fort Wayne, Edited by
        Michael Martone*
        By Michael Martone

No. 36 *Alien Stories*
        By E.C. Osondu

Colophon

BOA Editions, Ltd., a not-for-profit publisher of poetry and other literary works, fosters readership and appreciation of contemporary literature. By identifying, cultivating, and publishing both new and established poets and selecting authors of unique literary talent, BOA brings high-quality literature to the public. Support for this effort comes from the sale of its publications, grant funding, and private donations.

The publication of this book is made possible, in part, by the special support of the following individuals:

Anonymous (x3)
Anya Backlund, Blue Flower Arts
Angela Bonazinga & Catherine Lewis
The Chris Dahl & Ruth Rowse Charitable Fund
Sandra L. Frankel
Margaret Heminway
Kathleen C. Holcombe
Nora A. Jones
Paul LaFerriere & Dorrie Parini
Jack & Gail Langerak
Melanie & Ron Martin-Dent
Michael Martone & Theresa Pappas
Joe McElveney
Boo Poulin
Deborah Ronnen
Thomas Smith & Louise Spinelli
Elizabeth Spenst
William Waddel & Linda Rubel
Bruce & Jean Weigl